STEVEN FRAME—finally able to straighten out his confused, unhappy life, he is unable to stop the mysterious force that now threatens to tear it apart.

RACHEL DAVIS—to gain the love of the man she worships, she schemes to get rid of her unsuspecting husband.

RUSSELL MATTHEWS—his first marriage had ended in bitterness, his second would end in devastating heartbreak.

PAT RANDOLPH—affected by the tragedy of another marriage, she finds the strength to save her own.

———————

Story Editor **Mary Ann Cooper** is America's foremost soap opera expert. She writes the nationally syndicated column, *Speaking of Soaps*, is a major contributor and editor to leading soap opera magazines, and has appeared as a guest on numerous radio and television talk shows.

Martha Winslow, who wrote *Affairs of the Moment*, is a novelist and television writer who lives in New York City.

Dear Friend,

Can you remember the first time you were in love? It's as if it has never happened to anyone else in the world before. The joys of first love are exquisite, the pain is devastating. There is a part of each of us that never forgets the first time we were bitten by the love bug, and some of us are lucky enough to keep that love alive forever. Alice and Steve Frame knew that what they felt for each other was unlike anything they had known in the past.

Book 3, *Affairs of the Moment*, sadly reveals that even the greatest passion can cool. Yet Alice and Steve knew fate would bring them together again. Rachel, however, had other plans for Steve and would do anything to make him hers forever. Will Rachel's lies be her undoing? Not completely. Daytime villainesses have a way of landing on their feet. Look for Rachel's antics in many Soaps & Serials novels to come.

For Soaps & Serials Books,

Mary Ann Cooper

Mary Ann Cooper

P.S. If you missed Books 1 and 2 of this series, see the order form on page 192 which also tells you how to order books in our other Soaps & Serials™ paperback series.

ANOTHER WORLD

AFFAIRS OF THE MOMENT

PIONEER COMMUNICATIONS NETWORK, INC.

Affairs of the Moment

AS THE WORLD TURNS paperback novels are published and distributed by Pioneer Communications Network, Inc.

SOAPS & SERIALS™ is a trademark of Pioneer Communications Network, Inc.

ISBN: 0-916217-33-7

Printed in the United States of America

10 9 8 7 6 5 4 3 2 1

AFFAIRS OF THE MOMENT

Chapter One
A Question of Paternity

Alice Matthews sat in the hospital cafeteria drinking a cup of coffee and reading an item in the morning paper: "Dr. and Mrs. Russell Matthews announced the birth yesterday of a son, James Gerald Matthews, named for his two grandfathers, James Matthews and Gerald Davis. The baby, whose birth weight was three pounds, four ounces, is being kept in an incubator at Bay City's Memorial Hospital, where his father is a resident in internal medicine. Both baby and mother are doing well."

Alice, a tall, slender beauty with taffy-colored hair and a Dresden china look about her, pushed the coffee away. It left the same bitter taste in her mouth as the announcement. Try as she did to think how pleased and proud her brother, Russ, was to have a son, she couldn't push away the memory of his wife, Rachel, telling her Steven Frame was the baby's father, *insisting* that he was.

Alice wondered—not for the first time—if she was being fair to Russ in keeping his wife's infidelity from him. She had kept it from everybody at first. Nobody knew why Alice had broken her engagement to Steven, only that something had happened the night of the engagement party to cast some terrible shadow over it. Nobody had been privy to the scene in her bedroom when Rachel stormed in saying, "The man you're going to marry is the father of the child I'm going to have!"

Reeling from shock and disbelief, Alice had managed somehow to get through the party—and to face Steven with the accusation the next afternoon. She could still see him standing there, square-shouldered and square-jawed, an intensely masculine man with dark, brooding eyes. He admitted to having spent one night with Rachel at a time when he thought Alice was lost to him, when he was lonely and in despair. But he had vehemently denied being the baby's father.

Alice pushed away from the cafeteria table and headed back upstairs to the surgery wing. What she couldn't get over, and could never forgive Steven for, was his betrayal of her brother. *All right, so he was down and out and Rachel threw herself at him. He didn't have to let anything happen*, she reasoned. *He wasn't a child; he was a grown man. He knew what Rachel was like—and what she was after. How could he have been so stupid?*

Alice shook her head. She had been over and over it, rubbing at the wound as though it could be erased. All that she accomplished was to make herself feel worse than before, if that were possible. Better to push it out of her head altogether and lose herself in her nursing duties. If *that* were possible . . .

The surgery department was short-staffed, so she had little time for thinking about anything other than the work at hand. By the end of her shift she was tired and was grateful for the exhaustion she felt. What she didn't look forward to was going home to spend another long evening with her parents, the only alternative, for the time being, to spending evenings alone in her room. Not that there was any shortage of young men to go out with, but she wasn't interested in them and couldn't make herself be. Although she wouldn't admit it to anybody else and scarcely admitted it to herself, whether she forgave him or not, Alice was still very much in love with Steven Frame.

Before leaving the hospital she went to the premature nursery to see James Gerald Matthews. If Russ asked her about the baby she would be able to say she'd been to see him. There wasn't much to see. She peered through the viewing window, trying to find the tiny infant in the tangle of tubes and devices attached to his incubator.

Alice didn't linger—Rachel's room was down the hall, and she might appear at any moment. Worse, Russ might be with her, forcing Alice to put on a front of isn't-this-wonderful? But neither appeared before she made her escape.

At home her mother was in the kitchen getting dinner.

"Hi, honey." Mary Matthews smiled at her daughter. "Dad will be home soon. How was your day?"

"Busy . . . I looked in on the baby this afternoon. Have you been to see him yet?" Alice asked.

"We're going tonight," her mother answered. "I'm not looking forward to it, but as your father pointed out, Russ wouldn't understand why we were staying away, and how could we explain it?"

"How indeed?" Alice agreed. "I'm going upstairs, Mom, to change out of my uniform, and then I'll come down and help you with the rest of dinner."

* * *

In the weeks following her engagement party, Alice's parents had respected her privacy, not asking what had gone wrong, though plainly they wondered and worried. Finally, one night when her mother was out shopping for groceries, Alice told her father what had gone wrong. "But you mustn't tell Mom, Dad. She'd never be able to hide from Rachel how she feels about her."

"No," her father agreed, giving his daughter a gentle hug. "You're right."

But as time passed by, Jim Matthews turned the events over and over in his mind and decided it was unfair to mother and daughter to leave Alice's behavior unexplained.

As he expected, Mary was terribly upset when he told her. "I think we should keep quiet about all this," he said, trying to soothe her. "After all, there's no doubt in my mind that the baby is Russ's."

"Well," she said, "there *is* in mine."

"Now, darling, be reasonable. She spent one night with Steven Frame! She lives with Russ."

Mary Matthews sighed. "I see your point."

Alice saw it too. But why had Rachel been so adamant in saying the baby was Steven's? She had her chance to ask him one evening, when Steven, hoping for a reconciliation, arranged to meet her at a friend's house.

"Because she wants to believe it," Steven said. "She wants to make trouble for you, Alice. And for me as well. She'd like nothing better than to get her hands on some of my money. That's what this is all about."

"She says she loves you."

He grimaced. "Rachel would say black is white and believe it, if it would get her what she wants."

"She also said you love her."

"Well, I don't. You're the one I love, Alice. You and only you. Now and forever."

It broke her heart to hear him say it because she loved him too, but she couldn't bring herself to forgive him. Alice thought cynically that Rachel was fond of saying she never got what she wanted, yet if she had wanted to ruin her sister-in-law's life, she had done it.

As her husband had urged, Mary Matthews was keeping her emotions under control and wrestling with her conscience. And the more she wrestled, the more convinced she became that it wasn't fair to Russ to keep Rachel's betrayal from him. *As Rachel's husband he has a right to know,* she told herself. Finally, making up her mind to tell him herself, she called him at the hospital and asked him to drop by when he got off duty that night.

When he came into the kitchen she could hardly bear to look at him, but she steeled herself and was just on the verge of telling him about his wife's awful confession when the phone rang. It was Rachel's mother, Ada, looking for Russ.

"He's right here, Ada." She handed Russ the phone.

"Yes, Ada? What's up?"

"Russ, Rachel's starting labor."

His frown deepened. "Are you sure? She isn't due for two months yet."

"I know. But you know her history . . ."

He remembered Rachel's first pregnancy with dismay—the premature infant, stillborn—"Yes," he said tensely.

"The contractions are regular, Russ. I'm timing them. They're every ten minutes."

"Then you're right, Ada. I'd better meet you at the hospital."

And that put an end to the attempt to tell Russ what Rachel had done.

When Jim heard that Mary's plan had been thwarted, he sighed with relief. "What possible good could you have done?" he said to her. "You would only have made Russ miserable."

"I still think he has a right to know the truth."

"Darling, more than one truth is involved here. The most important is that Russ has a son, and he's very happy about it. Do you want to destroy that happiness?"

Alice's mother shook her head. "No."

"Well, then, there you are."

That conversation between her parents had taken place only this morning. Now, helping her mother set the table for dinner, Alice heard her father's car pull into the driveway. He came into the house with his briefcase full as usual with his accounting work, and with a big package.

"What's in the package?" she and her mother both asked eagerly.

"It's a present for Rachel. A red canvas tote." He put up a hand to forestall their objections. "Now, Mary, you know we have to go see Rachel and the baby, or find some good excuse to give to Russ. We also have to take her a present. We would under ordinary circumstances, wouldn't we?"

"I guess so, yes."

That put an end to the matter, at least for the moment.

While Jim and Mary Matthews were pretending to welcome their new grandson without any visible signs of doubt, they were preparing to welcome another grandchild in the next few months. No doubt whatever existed concerning this second grandchild's paternity. Their older daughter, Pat, was devoted to her lawyer husband, John Randolph, a tall, brown-haired, friendly-faced teddy bear of a man, and John was equally devoted to her. The only doubt about Pat's pregnancy preceded it.

Long before she met John, Pat had become pregnant by a boyfriend who didn't want to get married and talked her into having an illegal abortion—a messed-up job that supposedly had left her sterile. Then she met and married John; and when her obstetrician-gynecologist confirmed she was indeed pregnant again, Pat's joy knew no bounds. John felt exactly the same. At that moment if anybody had suggested to him he would soon be unfaithful to his wife, he would have called that person a liar.

One of John's most important clients was Steven Frame, or, more accurately, Steven Frame Enterprises. Starting with nothing more than his own ambition and knowhow, Steve had built up the multi-million-dollar conglomerate, with a construction firm as its centerpiece.

One day, after greeting John with his usual hearty handshake, Steve said, "Come here, John, I'd like you to meet my new administrator, Bernice Kline, a real winner. I can't tell you how glad I am she's working for us and not the competition!"

Bernice smiled. "I can't tell you how glad I am to be here!" she said, her eyes sparkling as they rested on John's open face. Not only did she enjoy working for Steve, she liked the life-style her salary provided. The only thing missing from her life now was a man, and she made up her mind at that moment to have John Randolph—wife or no wife.

Bernice had greeted the news that Pat was pregnant with outward congratulations and an inward shrug. From the experience of some of her women friends— she had no children of her own—Bernice knew there would be a time when, burdened by her swollen belly and various other aches and pains, Pat would become uninterested in sex. Then Bernice might be able to make her move. Her opportunity came sooner than she expected.

She was on the point of leaving John's law office one afternoon after taking him some papers when she ran into Pat, who was just coming in. Always on friendly terms with Pat, she said admiringly, "How marvelous you look!"

Pat smiled uncertainly. "You can't really mean that. I feel like a balloon."

Normally slender and elegant-looking, and blond like her sister, Alice, Pat had filled out considerably. Even Pat's face, usually so fine-featured, was a bit bloated.

"Well, you don't look like a balloon," Bernice said. "You look like a pregnant lady. John's very thrilled by that, I can tell you."

"I'm glad he's thrilled by something. He certainly isn't by the sight of me."

Bernice laughed. "You exaggerate, I'm sure. Well, I've got to get back to work. Nice to have seen you, Pat."

"Same here, Bernice. If I can work up the energy, I'll have you to dinner one night soon."

"Don't worry about it."

On the way home that evening Bernice thought about what Pat had said, wondering how much truth there was to it, and thinking maybe she ought to find out. The next morning, back in John's office, she mentioned seeing Pat, then added, "She seems to be having some difficulties with her pregnancy."

"Yes," he said, "she is. She's put on much more weight than the doctor expected her to. And she tires so easily. The doctor is beginning to suspect she might be carrying twins. He's going to check it out."

"Twins!" Bernice exclaimed. "Wouldn't that be something!"

"Yes, wouldn't it."

"You must be very excited, John."

"Yes," he agreed. "I am." But his voice had a curious lack of conviction.

In deciding to have John Randolph, Bernice assumed he could be had—and by her. Now she felt it was time to test that assumption. Taking the papers she had for him out of her briefcase, she set them down in front of him, her hand brushing and lingering against his. The response was electric. He jerked away, giving her a startled look.

"I'm sorry," she said. "I didn't mean to."

"No," John replied, ever the gentleman. "I'm sure you didn't. And I didn't mean to overreact. I'm sorry, Bernice."

"There's nothing to apologize for, John. Let's forget it."

"Yes, let's." But he gave her another look, not so much startled this time as disbelieving. Bernice felt a flutter of triumph—her assessment had been accurate. I'm going to have him! All I have to do is wait for the right opportunity, she thought.

Though she didn't have Pat's elegant good looks, Bernice was attractive enough to turn men's heads, and she had always been a stylish dresser. Now she began wearing more seductive clothes, garments that accented her shapeliness and the fashionably small size of her waist. Not much to her surprise, John noticed, though he didn't comment on it. She hadn't expected him to. It was enough that he noticed.

Even Steve Frame, troubled by his problems with Alice, noticed. "Who have you got designs on?" he asked one morning when she turned up at the office in a stunning, hip-hugging black wool dress.

"Nobody you know," she said. "You don't object to my clothes, do you?"

"Not as long as you keep them in good taste, no. And not as long as you're not after one of my clients."

"I'm not."

He shrugged. "Then go for it."

She smiled. "I intend to."

Steve eyed her narrowly. "Should I wish him luck?"

"Maybe."

He shook his head and went back to the set of plans he was working on.

Later the same day Bernice was with Steve when John brought him a number of papers to sign. "What do you think of our Mata Hari here?" Steve asked him.

"Very fetching," John answered. He was sure he sounded awkward saying it.

"Don't worry," Steve said. "She's not after any of us. She's going to spring her trap on some poor fellow in the outside world."

"I see." John began to look as uncomfortable as he sounded.

Bernice collected the proposal she'd been showing Steve. "I'll go on back to my own office, Steve, and finish showing you this later."

In the privacy of her office she smiled in anticipation.

On his way home that night John shook his head.

Steve might believe that Bernice had her sights on some outsider, but John knew better. She was gunning for him. She'd made that clear enough with her spine-tingling "accidental" touches, touches he no longer acknowledged and she no longer apologized for. And the clothes she wore—clothes that invited him, dared him. It gave him the sweats to think about it.

Well, he said to himself as he pulled into the driveway of his house, *then I won't think about it.*

Pat greeted him with a kiss, about all he got these days. He kissed her passionately in return, but she responded by pulling away and saying, "Darling, I can't. I'm just not up to it."

"Don't worry about it," he said. "It's okay. What can I do to help with dinner?"

"Nothing, really. It only has to be served. Why don't we have a drink first? I need to sit down and relax."

"You go do that. I'll make the drinks."

He did more than make the drinks. He served the dinner, cleared the table afterward, and filled the dishwasher.

After that he suggested a movie, but she didn't feel up to that either, so they spent the evening watching television, then went up to bed together. He tried another kiss there, but she put him off again.

Lying in bed sleepless a long time, he began thinking about Bernice. Then he thought about what Pat had told him about Rachel and Steve and what that had done to the Matthews family. He would not let that same thing happen to him. He would stay away from Bernice.

At last, he fell asleep, only to dream about her all night.

Chapter Two
Money and Desire

Everyone who knew Rachel was astonished at how she took to motherhood, even Russ. During her first pregnancy, the one ending in stillbirth, she had constantly complained that she didn't want to have a baby, she didn't like being pregnant, it was ruining her figure. During this pregnancy, however, she had been rapturous, and once the baby was born, proud and protective. When she was discharged from the hospital, the baby had to stay on until his weight reached five pounds. But once she had him home, there was no doubt who was in charge.

She herself had been abandoned by her father when she was only a baby. All through youth and adolescence, Rachel had devoted much time and energy to thinking about him, dreaming and fantasizing and making excuses for his abandonment—and, as time went on, making more excuses for his failure to contact either her or her mother, Ada, since. She'd even made some attempts to find him. From an old studio portrait of her parents, she got the name and address of the photographer in the town of Mount Holly. By calling Information, she learned he was still in the phone directory. But the address was only a storage depot, and she learned nothing more since that visit, made shortly after her marriage to Russ.

Russ was happy to see her so preoccupied with motherhood. Since their apartment had only one bedroom, Rachel put the baby in the living room at night and slept there with him, defending her behavior by saying the baby needed her with him in case something happened. He was, after all, still very tiny and prone to infection. Whether this was true or not, she wouldn't let anybody near the baby except her mother and Russ and, doctor or no doctor, even he was allowed to hold him only briefly.

But Russ tolerated her errant behavior, supposing that in time Rachel would relax and their life would become normal. Besides, if his domestic and social life was in chaos, his physical needs were more than satisfied. Rachel saw to that.

She had to. She wasn't going to walk out of a situation until she had a better one to walk into, and though she continued telling Steve at every opportunity that Jamie was his son and that he should take responsibility for him, Steve brushed her aside as being an opportunist.

"I don't know why you won't believe me, Steve," she said, turning up at his office one afternoon, unannounced as usual. "You're Jamie's father, and that's the truth."

"Rachel," Steve said, exasperated, "you wouldn't know the truth if you fell over it. Jamie is not my son. You've got to stop coming here this way."

Rachel thrust her chin up in a familiar gesture of

defiance. "Because you're ashamed to be seen with me?" Dark-haired, dark-eyed, with a heart-shaped face, she was extremely pretty and knew it.

"Because you have no business being here. What would Russ say if he knew?"

Rachel shrugged. "He doesn't know, so why worry about it?" Rachel's logic was her own.

"What if he calls you at the apartment?"

"Mom will tell him what I told her, that I left her with the baby while I went out to get a breath of fresh air . . . Speaking of the apartment, Steve, that's another reason I came to see you. Jamie needs a bedroom of his own."

Steve shrugged. "So get a bigger apartment."

"I intend to. I have one all picked out, only Russ says we can't afford it." What Russ had said was they couldn't begin to afford it on his salary as a resident and to forget about it. But Rachel had no intention of doing that.

"Then pick one out you can afford."

"But this one is perfect for Jamie."

Steve shook his head. "He's told you that, has he?"

Rachel's chin went up again. "There's no need for you to make fun of me, Steve. I only want what's best for our son, and you can afford to give him that."

"Rachel, for the last time, Jamie is not my son. If you think I'm going to help you pay for some fancy apartment you've got your eye on, think again." He got up from behind his desk and walked to the door of his office and opened it. "Now, if you'll excuse me, I've got work to do."

"Oh, all right," Rachel said, "but you needn't think you can forget about me, because I won't let you."

"Good-bye, Rachel."

Rachel hadn't really expected to get anywhere with

21

Steve, but she wasn't about to give up on the apartment she had set her heart on, either. She would simply have to find some other source of money for it.

Early in her pregnancy Russ's parents had talked about setting up a trust fund for each of their grandchildren. One morning as Russ and Rachel were getting dressed she said, "I wonder what bank the trust fund will be in."

Russ gave her a blank look. "What trust fund?"

There had been a time when any look from Russ set Rachel's pulse racing, for he was a handsome man, tall, slender, with a long, narrow face, dark hair, and dark eyes. But that was before Steve Frame came along, before his intense, brooding presence made Russ seem like a high school kid.

"The trust fund your parents talked about setting up before Jamie was born. Maybe you should remind them of it."

Russ shook his head. "Maybe I should, but I'm not going to. If they said they'll do it, they'll do it. The baby is only a few weeks old. Have patience, sweetheart."

Patience was something Rachel didn't have much of. On a night when Russ was on duty at the hospital, she invited herself for dinner with Jim and Mary. Skillfully, she worked the conversation around to the trust fund. "Remember," she said, "you talked about it back when I first got pregnant."

"Yes, we remember," Jim said.

Rachel put on her prettiest smile. "I guess you just haven't gotten around to doing anything about it yet. After all, as Russ said to me the other day, Jamie's only a few weeks old." Her smile brightened. "Russ also told me if you said you'd do it, you'd do it."

After Rachel and the baby had gone Mary fumed

about being blackmailed, saying she wasn't going to let Rachel get away with it.

Jim sighed. "I'm not sure we have any choice, darling. Other people know about the trust fund we promised them. What they don't know is the before and after—before we found out Rachel spent a night with Steven Frame and after we did. To them it's all Russ and Rachel and the baby. They'll be bound to wonder what made us back out, and Russ will wonder too."

"As far as I'm concerned," Mary said, "let them wonder. It's none of their business."

"And Russ?"

"We've already persuaded Russ to let us help him set up his private practice when his residency ends. With the money that's going to take he won't expect any more in the form of a trust fund. Anyhow, unlike some people I could mention, Russ has been too well brought up to prod his parents into doing something like this, let alone blackmail them into doing it."

"Well," Jim said, "we'll see."

A few days later Russ received an unexpected invitation from the federal government to participate in a medical study for the space program, an invitation that would take him to Houston, and keep him there for several weeks. No financial provision was made for the participants' wives, so Rachel was left behind, a situation that couldn't have suited her better.

"I'll never understand you, Rachel," her long-suffering mother said, arriving at the apartment to baby-sit. "You'd think Russ was so much dust under your feet."

"Those are your words, Mom, not mine. I would have been perfectly happy to go to Houston with Russ, but I wasn't invited."

"So you're perfectly happy to stay at home without him?"

Rachel tossed her dark head. "I intend to get some things done, yes."

"Things you don't want him to know about."

"Not in advance, no."

Ada looked her daughter straight in the eye. "What exactly are you talking about, Rachel?"

"Mom, when I've got it done, you'll be the first to know. Or at least among the first."

Her mother wasn't put off so easily. After all, she'd had long years of experience with Rachel and her schemes. "Are you talking about the trust fund, Rachel?"

"I am, if you must know."

Ada sighed. "I don't know how you have the gall to ask Jim and Mary Matthews to set up that trust fund for you."

"It's not for me. It's for Jamie."

"All right. For Jamie. I still don't see how you have the gall to do it."

Rachel shrugged. "They promised it."

"Yes, they did, when they thought the baby was their grandchild."

Rachel shrugged again. "As far as they know, he still is."

Her mother made a face. "That's what I mean by gall."

"Anyhow," Rachel said, readying her handsome new red canvas tote for an afternoon of shopping, "Jamie needs the money from that trust fund."

Ada frowned. "What for? What needs of Jamie's isn't Russ providing for?"

"I'm not talking about ordinary everyday things, Mom. I'm talking about, well, contingencies. You know. Like something comes up you're not expecting."

"Yes. I can think of something coming up that *you're* not expecting, Rachel, like Alice telling Russ the truth about you and Steven Frame. Are you prepared for *that* whatever-you-call-it?"

Rachel sighed. "I keep telling you, Mom, that's not going to happen. Do you think Alice wants to admit to anybody, especially to her beloved brother, that Steve prefers me over her?"

Ada shook her head. "What gives you that idea?"

Rachel pointed to the bedroom where Jamie slept during the day. "He does."

"Rachel, Steven Frame spent one night with you, and knowing you, you probably gave him no other choice. Has he said or done anything at all since then to make you think he prefers you over Alice?"

"Not exactly. Not yet."

"Not yet and not ever. Listen to me, Rachel. You take good care of the husband and the marriage you've got because that's the only one you're ever likely to have."

But like most of the sound advice Ada gave her daughter, it went in one ear and out the other.

When Jim told his son-in-law, John Randolph, to draw up whatever was necessary to establish the trust fund for Jamie, Alice found out about it and was appalled. "How could you do it?" she asked her father.

"Darling, I had no choice. Everybody in the family and around it knew about the trust fund. And," he added with a sigh, "Rachel's been reminding them of it, in case they'd forgotten."

"Naturally. She would. So you're rewarding her by giving her all this money."

Jim didn't want to hurt Alice any more than she already had been, and he said as much, reminding her,

"The money's not going to Rachel, honey. It's going to the baby."

"At this point it's the same." Alice's luminous blue eyes filled with tears. "First, she took my brother away from me, then the man I love, leaving me with nothing and her with money in the bank. It isn't fair."

And try as her father would to console and reassure her, she was neither consoled nor reassured.

The following afternoon Jim met Rachel in John's law office. "You understand," John said to both of them, "that until Russ gets back from Houston, Rachel is the sole trustee."

Jim nodded.

"Oh, my goodness," Rachel said, "you make me feel so important."

"Well," John said, "it is a responsibility being the trustee for all this money." His father-in-law had decided on an initial investment in the fund of $4,000, an amount that seemed to surprise Rachel. It seemed to please her, too, if please was the word. She had a feverish look, and John wondered if she was up to something—and if so, what?

She turned to Jim. "Mr. Matthews, I know you explained that this money is for Jamie later on, like when he goes to college. But . . .well . . .is there any restriction that says . . .I mean, if something should come up and we needed some money for Jamie then . . .well . . ."

"If something came up, Rachel, then of course you'd be able to draw on the fund. I guess you mean an illness or something like that."

Rachel looked more agitated than ever, but all she said was, "Yes, that's what I meant." John wondered again what she was up to. He didn't trust Rachel any more than anybody else in the family did. In fact, he had advised Jim not to set up the trust fund until Russ came back from Houston. People, however, had apparently been talking—gossiping—about the trust fund. Jim was tired of hearing about it and anxious to get the legalities over with. All that remained to be done was deposit the check in the bank, and since the bank stayed open late today, John decided he could get his secretary to take it there right away.

He ushered Jim and Rachel out of the office. As he was handing his secretary the check, Bernice arrived from Steve's offices, her briefcase bulging with documents.

By this time she excited such mixed emotions in him that he didn't know how he felt about seeing her, except that whenever she came to his office it irritated him. But it seemed to irritate him even more when she stayed away. At such times, he felt guilty for snapping at her, something entirely new in their relationship, and guiltier still for apologizing.

Then, when she brushed his fumbling accusations and apologies aside, as if they were not of the slightest importance, he was more irritated than ever.

Today he could afford to be courteous, affable even: Pat would be stopping by after her regular check up. Explaining that to Bernice, he invited her to sit down while he looked over the papers Steve had for him—in the same chair Rachel had occupied only a short while ago.

"Has Pat found out yet about the twins?" Bernice asked cordially.

"She expects to hear today."

"I wonder what it would be like to have twins."

John scribbled a note in the margin of one of the papers. "If the doctor's answer is yes, and both of us are expecting that now, you can ask me this time next year."

Bernice laughed. She had a husky, throaty laugh. Like everything else about her, it made him uncomfortable.

"In fact," he said, "we decided to go out tonight to celebrate our having twins."

Bernice frowned. "And if the doctor says it's only one baby?"

"Then we'll celebrate that!"

She laughed again.

John finished looking through the papers. "I only hope we haven't bitten off more than we can chew, as the saying goes."

Bernice looked up at him innocently. "So what have you bitten off?"

"Tonight we're having dinner at Tallboys, followed by the Frank Sinatra concert."

Her eyes grew wide. "How did you get tickets to that? It's been sold out for weeks."

"I've had the tickets for weeks. I wouldn't miss this for anything."

"I'm sure Pat is looking forward to hearing Ole Blue Eyes as much as you are."

"I don't have any doubt of that," John said, leaning back in his swivel chair and lacing his hands behind his head. "What concerns me is her staying power. I've told you how easily she tires."

Bernice nodded. "Yes. You have."

"The farther along she gets the more exhausted she becomes."

"When do you think she'll get here?" Bernice asked.

He glanced at his watch. "Oh, she should be along any minute now. Why?"

She smiled. "I'd kind of like to hear the doctor's verdict too."

"Be my guest," John said.

His secretary poked her head into his office. "I deposited the check, Mr. Randolph."

"Thank you."

"I was wondering. If you don't have any more dictation . . ."

"No, I don't."

"Would you mind then if I went home early?"

If Bernice weren't there, he wouldn't have minded at all. But he couldn't very well tell his secretary that. "No," he said. "I don't mind. Run along."

She beamed. "Thanks."

The office seemed intensely quiet after she left, except for the dim traffic noises drifting up from the street. John picked up the sheaf of papers Bernice had brought and riffled through them a second time, conscious he was doing "make-work," and conscious that Bernice knew he was.

"Would you rather I didn't stay?" she said into the silence.

He looked up from the papers and tried not to follow the plunging lines of the low-cut orange silk blouse she had on—another of her seductive outfits. Where in the devil was Pat? Before he could answer Bernice, Pat answered his mental summons. Hearing her come into the outer office, he breathed a sigh of relief.

"Hi, darling."

He greeted his wife in the outer office, leaning over to kiss her on the cheek. "What did the doctor say?"

Pat grinned at him. "He said what we expected. We're going to have two babies for the price of one. Though, come to think of it, he didn't say it that way." She walked with him into his office. "Hi, Bernice."

Bernice smiled. "Hi, Pat. Did John tell you I was waiting to hear the verdict?"

"No. But can you guess?"

29

"Twins?"

"Right."

"Double congratulations then."

"Thanks, Bernice." Pat sat down in the armchair next to her, and John went back to his accustomed seat behind the desk. Pat sighed. "Phew, that feels good! I never really understood before about sitting down to take a load off your feet, but I certainly do now."

"Are you tired, darling?" John asked.

She rested her head against the back of the chair. "I am—and have been for weeks now."

Bernice turned sympathetically to her. "Not too tired, I hope, for your evening out with your husband. He's been sitting here practically salivating over it."

Pat nodded. "Yes, I expect he has." She turned to John. "I'm sorry, darling. Really I am. But I don't think I'm up for tonight. Can you forgive me?"

"Oh, I'm sure he can," Bernice said before he had a chance to say anything. "The ones who won't be able to forgive you are all those disappointed Sinatra fans who weren't able to get tickets to his concert."

"It does seem a shame to waste them, doesn't it?" Pat said.

"You mean you'll change your mind about going?" John asked, hope stirring.

Pat shook her head. "No, darling. I'd like to. You know that. But I just can't manage it—that is, unless you want me to sleep through it."

"No, of course not. It's all right. What about dinner?"

"Oh, I can manage that." She turned to Bernice. "When it's a choice between being waited on or going home and waiting on myself, you can guess which one I'll choose."

"Well," Bernice said, getting to her feet, "since nobody's offering me that choice tonight, I'd better get on home."

Pat put out a protesting hand. "Have dinner with John and me."

Bernice smiled. "No. Thanks, Pat, but I didn't mean to sound like I was angling for an invitation."

"You weren't. But do have dinner with us. And then you can go to the concert with John. That way he'll be happy and the tickets won't go to waste." Pat smiled at John. "Is that all right, darling?"

How could he say that it wasn't? Besides, he did want to hear Sinatra. He wasn't making that up. "Yes, of course, darling. If Bernice has no objection."

Bernice smiled. "None at all."

So, after John called to change his reservation there from two to three, they set off for Tallboys. Throughout dinner Pat and Bernice chattered about the twins Pat was carrying—did they run in the family, would they be identical or fraternal, could Pat manage two infants on her own without outside help, had they thought about names, wouldn't Mary and Jim be thrilled to hear the news.

Finally Pat turned to John. "You haven't said much, darling."

"I don't know that I've been given the opportunity, but I think if we don't want to be late for the concert . . ."

Leaving the restaurant, John hailed a taxi and put Pat into it, tempted to get in with her and to hell with the concert. Let Bernice find somebody else to go with her. "Are you sure you'll be all right, darling? Say the word and I'll come home with you."

"Don't be silly. I'll be fine. You and Bernice enjoy yourselves."

"Well, all right." He shut the door and gave their address to the driver, then watched as the taxi moved off. He avoided looking directly at Bernice. "Shall we go then?"

She smiled. "Whatever you say, John."

The concert hall was packed, and the concert itself was all anyone could hope for. Sinatra was in glorious voice, his timing perfect, his songs the great standards from the thirties and forties. The audience ate it up, demanding encore after encore. Finally, it was over.

"I can't tell you how much I enjoyed that," Bernice said as they left the concert hall together.

"Yes. I did too," John said. "My car's in that garage over there. Come on, I'll drive you home."

She protested that he didn't have to. He insisted that he did. He couldn't very well put her in a cab and send her off alone this time of night. At last, she agreed to let him drive her home.

She was a perfumed presence all the way there—a perfumed, inviting presence, the silence between them as thick as the perfume. He felt as speechless—and as idiotic—as a kid on his first date.

Then the ride was over too, and he was escorting her to the door of her apartment building. She turned to thank him again for the evening, and before he knew what was happening, or how it had happened, she was in his arms, and he was kissing her with a depth of feeling which almost overwhelmed him. Dismayed, he broke away.

She smiled as if nothing had happened between them. "Goodnight, John." She turned her back on him and entered the building.

He stood staring after her. Maybe nothing had happened. Maybe he had only imagined it.

Chapter Three
A Case of Amnesia

The day after Jim Matthew's check was deposited in the bank, Rachel did two things. First, she went to the rental agent to tell him she and her husband were taking the apartment he had shown her. However, since her husband was out of town and wouldn't be back for five or six weeks more, could it be held for them until then?

The rental agent opened his ledger. "I'll be happy to hold it for you," he said, "but first you'll have to give me one month's rent and one month's security, a total of eight hundred and fifty dollars."

Rachel tried to hide her dismay. "Well, yes, of course. I mean, well, first I'll have to write my husband and get him to send it to me. That will probably take a few days, so . . . I mean, can you hold it for us until then?"

The building was new, the apartment Rachel had her heart set on in its G line. "There are five of those apartments left," the agent said. "I'm sorry, but it's first come, first served."

Rachel hurried from the new building to the bank, intending to take the money from the baby's trust fund. "I'm sorry," the teller there told her, "no funds in any amount can be withdrawn until after thirty days."

Stunned, Rachel returned to her old apartment to try to think what to do next.

She called her mother to come baby-sit for her. While waiting for Ada to arrive, she wrote a letter to her father at the storage-depot address, asking him for the $850.

Ada was appalled at the idea. "You think your father's going to send you money when he hasn't even bothered getting in touch with you all these years?"

"Maybe he will," Rachel said, fingering the envelope.

"Yes," Ada agreed, "and maybe tomorrow the sun will come up in the west. And where are you off to at this time of day?"

Rachel gave her a disgusted look. "Mom, you make it sound like it's the middle of the night when it isn't even noon yet."

"That isn't telling me where you're going or why you can't take Jamie with you instead of dragging me over here."

"I explained that to you on the phone. I've already had him out all morning with me, and I'm having lunch with Lenore at Tallboys. I can't very well take Jamie there."

"Oh, all right," Ada said.

Rachel wasn't having lunch with Lenore. In fact, she was hoping to have lunch with Steve, knowing he frequently ate lunch at Tallboys. She was in luck, at least initially.

"Go away, Rachel," he said, looking up from the steak he was eating. "I don't want you at my table."

She smiled her prettiest smile. "Would you rather have a scene?"

He sighed and nodded to the chair across from him. "Sit down then. What is it this time?"

She sat down and clasped her hands together on the white linen tablecloth. "Steve, I have to have eight hundred and fifty dollars."

"Ask your husband for it."

"You know he hasn't got that kind of money."

He cut a piece of steak and chewed it slowly. "What's the money for, Rachel?"

"It's for Jamie's new apartment. I need one month's rent and one month's security."

Steve put his knife and fork down and stared at her. "I've always known you weren't a mental giant, Rachel, but I did think you had some sense. If Russ doesn't have the eight-fifty for the first and last month's rent, how is he going to come up with the money for the months in between?"

"I'll worry about that later."

He shook his head and went back to his steak. "You and Scarlett O'Hara."

"Please, Steve. I'm only asking to borrow the money."

"Forget it, Rachel. I've had all the dealing with you I ever intend to have."

A waiter approached the table with a menu. Taking it, Steve handed it to Rachel and got to his feet. "Let me amend that slightly. Have lunch on me, Rachel." Steve nodded pleasantly and left the restaurant.

Rachel did have lunch on him, and had another bit of luck as well. As she was leaving Tallboys, she ran into Liz Matthews, Russ's wealthy aunt, coming in. Again putting on her sweetest smile, Rachel said, "Oh, Mrs. Matthews, I'm so glad to see you. You said to let me know when Russ's parents set up the baby's trust fund so you could contribute, and they did it yesterday."

Liz of course hadn't said in so many words that she would contribute to the baby's trust fund, but she didn't want to get into an argument with Rachel in the middle of Tallboys. With as much graciousness as she could muster, which wasn't much, she sat down at a nearby table and wrote out a check for a hundred dollars. When her luncheon companion joined her there and saw what she was doing, she insisted on writing out a check for a hundred dollars for the baby's trust fund too.

Rachel took both checks directly to the rental agent as proof of her intention. "Until my husband has a chance to hear from me and write me back," she said, again summoning up her prettiest smile.

"First come, first served," the agent reminded her.

That still left her $650 short. A couple of days later she ran into the very pregnant Pat in Bryant's Department Store. Pretending she had lost her wallet with fifty dollars in it, and summoning up tears this time, she managed to get fifty dollars in cash from Pat.

A few days after that, when her mother was at the grocery store, Rachel got twenty-five dollars out of her on the pretext that Russ had left her short of money.

The seventy-five dollars also went to the rental agent.

After that she began watching the mailbox for word from her father, but no word came. Nor was she able to worm anymore money from any other person on any pretext whatever. So she was reduced to crossing her fingers and holding her breath until the rest of the thirty days went by. Then she went to the bank and drew the remaining $575 from Jamie's trust fund, practically running from the bank to the rental agent. Two G-line apartments were still available.

When she returned home, the phone was ringing. Leaving Jamie in his buggy, she picked up the receiver, thinking maybe it was her father calling.

"Hi, Rachel." It wasn't her father; it was Russ.

"Oh. Russ. Where are you?"

"I'm still in Houston. But that's why I'm calling. I'll be home Friday."

"Friday?" she said, dismayed. "You mean this Friday?"

"Yes."

"But Russ, that's only three days from now."

"I know it is and I'm pleased as punch. I thought you would be too."

"Russ, of course I am. It's just that . . . well, I have this surprise for you, and I . . ."

"What surprise?"

"Russ, if I told you, it wouldn't be a surprise, would it?"

"No, I guess not."

"And I don't see how I possibly can have it ready for you by Friday."

"It must be some surprise."

"It is. Oh, darling, you're going to love it. But now I've got to get off the phone and get moving. I mean . . . well, never mind what I mean. I almost gave the surprise away."

Barely giving him time to tell her when to meet him at the airport, she hung up the phone.

She picked it up immediately and called a moving company, hung up again, and began packing, scrounging for boxes from every liquor store and supermarket in the neighborhood. By working harder than she'd ever worked before and concentrating totally on the move, she made it in the three short days allotted to her, even managing to get the new apartment all set up.

Meeting Russ at the airport Friday afternoon, she drove him to the new address, and together they rode up in the elevator to 15G. "Why don't we go home first?" Russ kept asking. "Can't the surprise wait?"

Inside the apartment he stared at their familiar furnishings in this unfamiliar place, and the nature of her "surprise" sank in. He was stunned at first and then angry when he realized that this was the apartment he'd already told her they couldn't begin to afford and to forget about it.

"Where did you get the money for it?" he demanded.

"I didn't get it. I had it. I must say, Russ, you're not being very nice about this."

"What do you mean, had it? Don't you think I know how much money we have? Where did you get the money, Rachel?"

"Well, if you have to know, I got it from the baby's trust fund and from some money your Aunt Liz gave me to put into it."

Russ couldn't believe he was hearing her correctly. "You took your own baby's money for this ridiculous, extravagant apartment? You let my parents and Aunt Liz and God knows who else think they were giving money to Jamie for his future? That's embezzlement, Rachel, pure and simple."

That was hardly the end of it. Realizing how costly it would be to break the new lease and move to yet another apartment, Russ was forced to ask his parents for help in paying the rent until he and a colleague got settled into private practice together. Then he laid down the law to Rachel, curtailing her spending and removing her name from the trust fund altogether. He told Rachel if she couldn't accept his rules she could have the apartment all to herself.

"I'm surprised," her mother sniffed after hearing a blow-by-blow account from Rachel, "he didn't kick you out of here." Ada didn't think much of the new apartment either, calling the building a glass cookie box.

Rachel threw back her pretty, dark head. "He'll get over being mad in a few days. And meanwhile I got what I wanted, didn't I?"

"Yes, you did," Ada agreed. "For now."

Meanwhile, Alice was trying to make a new life for herself. Late one afternoon, as she was getting ready to go out to dinner with a new date, Russ called her from Bay City Memorial's emergency room. "We've got a bad accident case coming in, Alice. The guy's got head injuries and he's in a coma. The ambulance just phoned in and so did the nurse assigned here. I mean she phoned in sick. Can you possibly give me a hand until I can get a replacement?"

"Sure, Russ. I'll be right there," she answered reassuringly.

The accident victim turned out to be Steven Frame. He had fallen at one of his construction sites and injured his head. Alice blanched when Russ broke the news. "I'll try to get another nurse as fast as I can," he said.

Alice shook her head. "No. I'll stay and take care of him."

Not much was required of her that night. She spent most of it in the hall outside an operating room while a neurosurgeon removed the blood clot that had formed after the skull was fractured, relieved the pressure on the brain, and stopped the intracranial bleeding. After that it was wait and see.

Russ persuaded her to go home for what was left of the night. "Otherwise, you won't be fit for tomorrow. That's when you can really be useful."

Alice was back at Steven's bedside at seven-thirty the next morning. He still hadn't regained consciousness, but a night nurse reported that in his restless tossings he'd been calling her name all night.

When she entered the room, he opened his eyes, but only for a second, and without apparent recognition. He did it again. And again. Finally, he opened his eyes and looked at her. "Hello, Steven," she said softly. Her heart speeded up when he nodded in reply. "Do you know where you are?"

"Hospital?" he said hoarsely.

"Yes, Steven. And do you know who I am?"

"Alice." His voice quavered.

"Alice who?"

He tried to smile. "There's only one Alice." His voice was still shaky but stronger. "My Alice. My darling." Under the bedding his hand moved. "Hand? Hand. Your hand."

She held out the hand that was nearest—her left. He took it and squeezed it, then frowned. "No ring. Where's your ring?"

"Ring?" she said, startled. "What ring?"

He spoke with effort. "The one I gave you. Your engagement ring. Why aren't you wearing it?"

The neurosurgeon had said there might be temporary paralysis or memory loss. Was it possible he—?

"Why aren't you wearing it?" he asked again. "You promised you'd never take it off."

Afraid of upsetting him when he was in such a mentally fragile state, she answered, "Steven, I know what I promised. But I've been working with some strong antiseptics, and I didn't want to damage it."

Her reply seemed to satisfy him, and he drifted off again.

When Russ came in, Alice took him aside and told him what had happened.

"I see," he said, then stood there thinking. After several moments' silence, he said, "Alice, I've never asked why you broke your engagement to Steve, and I'm not asking now. But can you tell me this much? Did he want to break it?"

"No. It was my doing."

"Well, there's your answer then. The blow to his head blotted out the memory of something he wanted to forget. Apparently your breakup caused him a great deal of anguish, so much so that now his mind refuses to accept it."

"But he'll have to remember sometime, Russ."

"Yes. When he's stronger. When he's able to accept it. He'll gradually recover a bit here, a bit there, until finally most of the pieces of the puzzle will be back in place."

"In the meantime?"

"That depends on you. He'll get well faster if you can play along with him. But if you can't bring yourself to do that—and believe me, I'll understand if you can't—then I'll make some excuse to Steve and take you off the case."

She shook her head. "No. He likes having me take care of him, and that will help him get better too. No. I'll play along with him."

Russ gave her a look of such tender concern she almost broke down. "Are you sure you can handle this, Alice?"

She blinked back her tears. "Yes, I'm sure."

But she wasn't at all sure and that night, telling her

father what had happened, she did break down. "He asks me over and over if I love him, Dad, makes me promise I'll never leave him."

Her father put an arm around her. "Darling, what a terrible strain all this pretending must be for you."

She shook her head. There were tears on her cheeks. "It isn't pretending when I say I love him, Dad. I do love Steven. I always have."

The next day Steven wanted to talk to her about their dream house. They had discussed it for hours on end during their engagement—an old-fashioned two-story house in the country, a room for them and for each of the children, a house with floor-to-ceiling draperies at its many, many windows, and outside the windows lay the tree-dotted countryside.

In the first days after Steven's accident, they built it again, and talked about the plans they had made for their life together. Steven was still bothered by the absence of her ring. He came back to the subject repeatedly, first seeming to accept her explanations, then asking her again why. One afternoon he said, "Why can't you wear it around your neck on a chain if you can't wear it on your finger?"

Thinking a bit, she said, "Maybe I could, Steven, but I'd have to find the right chain for it. How can I do that and take care of you?"

Again he seemed satisfied.

For some days after Steve's accident he was not allowed any visitors, so Rachel fumed and fretted about him in her fancy new apartment for which she'd sacrificed so much. *Look at the good it's doing me now*, she pouted. There were loads of things the apartment needed, but would Russ let her buy any of them? Fat chance. And then Ada had to come by one morning and drop her bombshell. "I've just heard," she said, "that Steven Frame thinks he's still engaged to Alice."

"He what?" Rachel said, furious. "Why didn't Russ tell me?"

"Because it's none of your business."

"I'll make it my business."

That afternoon she sneaked into the ward to visit Steve and found him alone in his room. He didn't pretend he was happy to see her there. "My fiancée is taking care of me," he said. "I don't need you here. Or want you either."

Rachel laughed. "Your fiancée? Alice? Is that what she's calling herself? Your fiancée?"

He frowned at her. "Not calling herself. Is. I'm going to marry Alice, Rachel."

Rachel laughed again. "Is she saying that too? What kind of games are you two playing?"

He gave her a bewildered look. "I don't play games, Rachel. You do. Like the game about your baby."

Her expression hardened. "That's not a game, Steven. That's the truth. Jamie is your baby. Yours and mine."

"Go away, Rachel."

"You can't make the truth go away, Steven. Somebody needs to straighten you . . ."

Before she could finish the sentence, Alice came into the room. And before she could draw another breath, Alice had yanked her out into the hall. "You listen to me, Rachel. Steven is a very sick man."

"Sick?" Rachel countered. "He's out of his mind. Those fantasies about the two of you."

"Exactly," Alice said. "Fantasies. That's what they are. And until he gets well, we're all going along with him. Everybody, including me. You're going to go along with it too, Rachel, by staying away from here. If

you don't, I'm going to tell Russ about you and
Steven. Do you understand?"

"I don't believe you."

"Try me and see."

Rachel didn't visit Steve again.

Steve's accident had other aftereffects. John Randolph
had to spend more time at Steven Frame Enterprises,
looking after its various interests. Steve had other
executives besides Bernice, but John more or less took
over as chief, making the decisions Steve would
normally make, entertaining clients, looking into new
business opportunities.

Though John knew it wasn't deliberate, Steven
seemed to be aiding and abetting Bernice's plot. When
he was well enough to talk business, Steve would bring
up something, then say, "Ask Bernice about it." Or
"Get Bernice to show you where that file is." Or "See if
Bernice knows what date we gave on that
construction job."

John found himself spending more and more time
with Bernice, who made no secret of her pleasure at
being with him. Remembering what happened after
the Sinatra concert and not wanting it repeated, even
though he couldn't put it or her out of his mind for
long, John did his best to keep his distance. However,
she frustrated him constantly, leaning over his
shoulder to look at something, her hand resting on his
wrist or shoulder. Once as they were riding together in
a crowded elevator, in the guise of being pushed by
another rider, she turned toward him and pressed
herself against him, her breasts pressing against him,
making his pulses throb. Bernice, Bernice, Bernice. He
was going crazy, and crazy with desire for her.

One spring afternoon he was in Steve's office

working at his massive mahogany desk, when Bernice came in with some blueprints she wanted to file. The day was unusually warm, and Bernice was dressed in a tomato-red cotton dress that clung to her slim waist. The spaghetti straps at her shoulders barely contained her surging breasts. John tried not to look at her, forcing himself to concentrate instead on the papers before him.

One wall of Steve's office was lined with shelves that held many of the company's files. She needed a small step stool to reach the shelf she wanted and somehow—since he was deliberately not watching her, he didn't know how—it slipped from under her, leaving her dangling and calling for help from an avalanche of paper.

"Hold tight," John said. He held her around the waist and lifted her safely down. She stood there clinging to him.

It was too much. His mouth sought hers and she responded, leaning into him, setting his blood on fire. He pulled away, but only long enough to look at her before seizing her again. His tongue explored her mouth. His hand pushed the thin straps down to fondle her surging breasts, his heart pounding in his chest.

Where it would have gone from there he didn't know, for he wasn't thinking. The phone rang.

Even as he crossed to Steve's desk to pick it up, Bernice straightened her dress. She knew as well as he did that the spell was broken. For the time being . . .

"John?" It was his mother-in-law. Pat was so near term he had left a battery of numbers both with Pat and with Mary where he could be reached—his office number, Steve's, the club where he ate lunch.

"Yes, Mary. Is it Pat?"

"Yes. She started having contractions about an hour ago. I've phoned her doctor and he said to come on in."

"I'll meet you at the hospital then, unless you want me to—"

"No, no, meet us there."

He didn't bother putting the papers on Steve's desk together. "Leave them there," he told Bernice. "I'll come back to them."

"Good luck!" she called to him as he left the office. All thought of her was gone from his head now. His only concern was Pat and the twins she would be having before this day was over. He prayed God wouldn't punish him for his transgressions by taking it out on his wife or their babies.

Two and a half hours later Pat gave birth to a boy and a girl. Both were healthy and beautiful. John hugged Mary and Jim and Russ and Alice and everybody else in sight. From now on, he promised himself, he would be the husband his wife deserved, not the mental, and nearly physical, adulterer he'd been lately.

Like many new mothers, Pat went into postpartum depression a few days after the twins' birth. She was either always on the verge of tears or else the tears flowed copiously `at a careless word or gesture. The doctor explained that Pat's condition was not psychological but physical and was caused by the sudden cessation of hormones her body had been infused with during the pregnancy. In a few days the depression would pass.

Only it didn't.

Shortly before Steven Frame was to be discharged from the hospital, to be cared for at home by private nurses, his memory began to return. It happened the way the neurosurgeon and Russ had predicted it would—he would get a hazy idea or mental picture that, over the course of a few hours or a day, would become clearer, more definite, and then he would remember what had been a blank to him before.

It happened in other ways too. One morning, stopping by on rounds, Russ mentioned to Steve that he too would soon be leaving Memorial Hospital to open a clinic with an obstetrician-gynecologist colleague, Dan Shearer.

Surprised that Russ's residency was so near its end, Steve said, "It seems so sudden." He shook his head. "I get this feeling that there's a gap in my life—a whole period of time I don't remember."

"What makes you think that?" Russ asked.

"I don't know. People. Bits of conservation. And Alice. Mostly Alice."

When he didn't go on, Russ prompted him. "What about Alice?"

Steve sighed. "When she leaves the room, I get the uneasy feeling she isn't coming back, that she isn't ever coming back." He shook his head. "I know it sounds crazy. It is crazy, because she's never gone for more than a few minutes at a time, but still I feel as if she's lost to me forever."

When Alice came back to the room, Russ took her aside and told her what was happening. "It's all going to come back to him, Alice, and soon. Brace yourself."

The day before his discharge Steve said to Alice, "I'll go home on one condition—that you'll come visit me every evening and on your days off. Will you promise?"

"Yes, Steven. I promise."

He gave her a look of such pain her heart

contracted. "Steven, what is it? What's the matter?"

He shook his head. "I don't know. I have this terrible feeling, and I can't figure out why. What is it, Alice? What am I forgetting?"

"Don't worry about it, Steven," she said breezily.

But he worried about it on and off all day. Then there were the dreams that had begun tormenting him all night. "I've had some of the damnedest dreams. There's one about blasting, and one about a party. And something after the party that I didn't like."

The more he went on about the dreams and the bits and pieces of conversation that were coming back to him, the more upset he became. Alice tried to calm him. "Don't worry yourself, Steven. Please. It will be all right."

"But that's what bothers me," he said. "I'm worried it won't be all right. Something somewhere is terribly wrong. I think I've done something to hurt you." He gave her a pleading look. "What have I done, Alice?"

"Nothing, Steven. Nothing."

The look intensified. "Alice, you do still love me, don't you?"

She squeezed his hand. "Yes, darling, I do. I swear it."

"And even though you can't wear your ring here at the hospital, we are engaged, aren't we?"

"Yes, Steven, we are. Please, darling, you mustn't think about it."

When her shift ended in the afternoon, she was tempted to stay on, fearful that leaving him would upset him further. Yet since he knew it was time for her to go, maybe her staying on would upset him more. Finally she left, saying she would see him in the morning when she would help him get ready to leave the hospital.

The next day she was back in his room at seven-thirty, helped him shave and wash up, served him his breakfast, and was dismayed when he wouldn't eat it. "You have to eat, Steven. You must get your strength back."

"What I have to get back," he said tersely, "is my memory."

"Don't worry about it. It will come back. Now please eat your breakfast."

He toyed with it.

A short time later a messenger arrived with a suitcase Steve's secretary had packed for him. In it, she had packed some clothes to wear home. Alice helped him dress.

Buttoning his shirt, Steve asked, "Did she send cuff links?"

"I don't know." Alice said. "I'll look in your jacket." In the pocket was a small jewelry box. "Yes. Here they are." She handed it to him.

He opened it. Inside with the cuff links was Alice's engagement ring. He stared at it, then gave her a bewildered look. "It's your engagement ring. But you said—" He broke off and bewilderment changed to horror. "Oh, my God. I remember." He sank down on the bed and buried his face in his hands. "I remember everything."

Chapter Four
The End of a Marriage

Even before the Randolph twins were born, Pat and John had been looking for a live-in nursemaid to help relieve Pat of the physical burden of taking care of two infants. After interviewing a number of applicants they settled on an attractive young woman named Caroline, who had a good deal of experience with infants. Soon she relieved Pat entirely of the child care.

It was probably just as well. Although Pat loved the twins, Michael and Marianne, and was proud to show them off to anybody and everybody, her postpartum depression lingered on. Her mother urged Pat to consult her obstetrician. "I'm sure he can prescribe something for you that will help, Pat."

"I'm sure he probably can too, Mother, but I don't want to start taking pills and then get dependent on them. This will pass. I need a little more time, that's all."

She said much the same thing to her husband when he too urged her to see a doctor. After she'd been home from the hospital for a few weeks and John took her in his arms one night in their bedroom as a preliminary to making love, she turned away from him, saying, "Darling, I can't. Not yet. I need more time."

"Maybe you just need a change of scene," John said, stroking her hair. "We could go to the Caribbean for a few days—Steve has that house in St. Croix. I'm sure he'd let us use it. He's very generous about offering it to his friends."

"Yes, I know, but I don't like leaving the babies for that long, John."

"Caroline is so good with them."

"Yes, she is, but still I don't want to leave them. You go to St. Croix if you want to."

Taking off his shirt and tie, he frowned at her. "What fun would that be without you?"

"I'm not much fun for you here."

"Darling, it's all right. I know what you've been through. I understand." He took her in his arms again and she let him comfort her, but when his kiss turned passionate she slipped away from him. "John, I've already told you. I can't. Not yet."

He swallowed his frustration and tried to think of other ways to divert her. The next day, while he was eating lunch at his club, another lawyer stopped by his table to say that he and his wife had driven to Somerset last night to have dinner in that restaurant everybody was talking about, the Riverboat. He thought it was well worth the drive.

"How far is it?" John asked.

The man shrugged. "About half an hour's drive. But you'd better call first and make a reservation, or you might make the drive for nothing."

When he returned to his office, John called the restaurant and made a reservation for that evening, then he phoned Pat to tell her what he had done. He half-expected her to object; but she was in a somewhat brighter mood and acted pleased.

As John's colleague had reported, dinner at the Riverboat was worth the drive there and back. However, it didn't change the outcome in John and Pat's bedroom later that night when once again he tried to make love to her. "I'm sorry, darling," she said. "I know how much you want to. And I do too—honest I do. But I can't. Not yet."

That night he began dreaming of Bernice again.

If dinner at the Riverboat did nothing for John's love life, it had stunning repercussions for a visitor to the Randolph household the following day. Rachel came to see Pat and the twins, and Pat mentioned how pleasant the new restaurant was.

"Oh," Rachel said, "I've been dying to get Russ to take me there, but he won't. He says he—hasn't got the time." She had been about to say, "He can't afford it," but she supposed the whole Matthews family knew about the fuss over the apartment and the mean budget Russ had imposed on her. Anyhow, she'd never paid Pat back the fifty dollars. "Does it really look like a riverboat?"

"More or less," Pat said. She fished in her purse for the paper matchbooks she'd brought home. "Here," she said, handing Rachel one, "this will give you some idea."

Rachel gazed admiringly at the drawing on the cover, then opened it to see what might be inside. She gasped.

Pat looked concerned. "What is it Rachel? What's the matter?"

For once Rachel had been struck dumb. She held the open matchbook out to Pat. Printed on the inside cover was, "Gerald Davis, Proprietor." Finding her voice she said, "That's my father. It has to be."

Pat said skeptically, "But I thought your father was in Mount Holly."

"No. He only has a storage depot there. Oh, I've got to go to Somerset and see him." She rose quickly from the sofa she'd been perched on.

Pat protested, "But surely you don't mean you're going right this minute."

"No. It'll take me an hour or so to make arrangements for Jamie and to see what the bus schedule is."

"But, Rachel, have you forgotten about tonight?"

Rachel gave her sister-in-law a blank look.

"Tonight is the reception at the clinic. You surely don't want to miss that. This is a big night for Russ—the real beginning of his medical career."

"Yes, I know that."

Russ and his ob-gyn colleague Dan Shearer were opening their new clinic tomorrow, and tonight they were hosting a reception there.

Pat held up the matchbook. "If this Gerald Davis really is your father, fine. But he'll still be there tomorrow. You can go then."

"Well," Rachel said, "maybe, but I still have to go home and start making arrangements. No, don't get up, Pat. I can see myself out."

Rachel hurried home. Her "maybe" had been only a sop to Pat. She was determined to go to Somerset today, whether Russ liked it or not. He didn't need her at the clinic, and it was all she could do to conceal her contempt for it. She had thought that once out of his residency and into a private practice, Russ would finally become the wealthy man she had thought she'd married. But no. He was too pure and noble to care about money. He and Dan Shearer were going to run a low-fee clinic, and she and Russ would still be scraping along years from now. It infuriated her to no end.

After parking Jamie with her mother, she went to the clinic, where Russ and Dan were overseeing the finishing touches for the night's festivities. She showed Russ the matchbook and told him she was taking the two o'clock bus to Somerset. "You don't mind, do you, Russ? You know how much this means to me."

Russ could have said the same to Rachel regarding the clinic, but he didn't. He had learned that when her mind was made up, arguing with her was a waste of time.

So she went off to Somerset and to the Riverboat, only to learn when she got there that her father, if indeed this Gerald Davis was her father, had left for the day.

"But what about tonight?" Rachel asked the bartender. "Won't he be back tonight?"

The bartender shook his head. "No, ma'am. He isn't due back till tomorrow morning."

Disappointed but determined not to leave Somerset until she met with Gerald Davis, Rachel checked into a motel. Fortunately she'd considered that she might be spending a night or two here, so she'd brought all the household money with her. She'd deal with Russ about that when she had to. Her father would probably give her the money anyhow.

Bright and early the next morning she was back at the Riverboat. A different bartender said yes, Gerald Davis was there, but he had someone with him in his office. If she'd care to wait . . .

Rachel sat down with a sigh at one of the tables. Nearby a blond girl was leafing through a magazine, apparently waiting for someone too. After several minutes a dark-haired, dark-eyed, middle-aged man with a slight paunch came up to Rachel. "Are you the young lady who was asking for me?"

A thrill shot through Rachel. "Are you Gerald Davis?"

"Yes. Can I help you?"

Before she could answer, the blond girl said, "Excuse me, Pops, but I have to talk to you about the swimsuit you promised me."

Rachel scarcely heard her or what her father—it had to be him—said in reply, something about this other young lady was here to see him. He turned back to Rachel. "Are you here about a job? I'm afraid we don't . . ."

"I'm not here about a job. I'm your daughter. I'm Rachel."

The blond turned to stare at her. "Hey, Pops," she said.

Rachel heard her clearly this time. She frowned. "Why does she call you Pops?"

The girl answered for him. "Because he's my father."

Now Rachel stared. "Your father?"

"Well, yeah. I mean, what did you think?"

Rachel, taken aback, had no answer. Her father turned to the girl and said, "You'll have to excuse me for a while longer, Pammy." To Rachel he said, "Why don't you come into my office? We can talk there."

One wall of his office was covered with photographs of the girl, Pammy, at different periods of her life. Rachel looked for even one picture of herself, but there was none. Seating her in front of his desk, her father took his place behind it. "I'm sorry," he said, "for not ʻ... ʌing you up all these years. I meant to, but . . . well . . ." His voice trailed off.

"Why didn't you?" Rachel asked. She had always

assumed her father had had some good reason for not getting in touch with her, something to do with her mother, she was sure.

"Oh, no reason really," he said casually, dashing that assumption. "I was on the bum for a while. Then I met my second wife, and Pammy came along and . . . well . . ." His voice trailed off again.

"But you are so near to me here in Somerset."

He nodded. "Yeah. Funny, isn't it?"

To Rachel it was anything but funny. She took a picture of Jamie out of her tote and handed it to him. "You have a grandson, and he's named for you. James Gerald Matthews."

Her father looked at the picture and handed it back. "He's a handsome baby. And your husband?"

"He's a doctor. Dr. Russell Matthews."

"Rachel, that's fine. You've done very well for yourself."

"Yes, I suppose I have. But that doesn't mean I don't have problems a father can't help me with, and that's one of the reasons I'm here—to get to know you—and you me—so you can be a father to me. So you can talk to me and give me advice."

Her father smiled uncomfortably. "I'm afraid I'm not much of an advice giver, Rachel. You'd be better off going to your husband for that."

She frowned. "But what if the advice I want has to do with my husband?"

"Then I guess you'll have to go to your mother. She knows you a lot better than I—"

The bartender stuck his head in the door. "Sorry to interrupt, but there are some deliveries coming in you have to sign for."

Her father stood up. "I'll be back in a few minutes, Rachel."

Soon he was back, but each time she tried to get a real conversation going, there'd be another interruption—the bartender or somebody on the phone. Finally her father said to her, "I'm afraid it's going to be like this the rest of the day now. You'll have to excuse me."

"Sure," Rachel said, getting up. "But when can I see you again?"

"Any time you're in the neighborhood. How about you and your husband coming over for dinner some night?"

Rachel's fading hopes recovered slightly. "Why, yes, we'd like that."

He smiled. "And if I ever get to Bay City I'll look you up."

Her wan hopes flickering, she could barely hide her disappointment. "Yes, do that."

"Oh, and before you go, Rachel—take these." He gave her two Riverboat ashtrays, a bottle of cheap perfume, and a lobster bib for Jamie. "Don't forget," he added. "If you and your husband do get over here for dinner, everything's on the house. Okay?"

Unable to answer him, she nodded and left.

One of Russ's first clinic patients was a young woman named Cindy Clark, a quiet, gentle, dark-haired girl with a mild but chronic heart condition. Because of it Russ advised her to avoid physical and emotional stress in her work. In response she smiled shyly and gave him the want-ad she had cut from the morning paper. It was the ad he and Dan Shearer were running for a receptionist.

Russ flashed an answering smile, saying, "The job is yours."

She turned out to be perfect for it—courteous to the

patients, efficient at filing and billing, and always ready to do whatever was asked of her.

She was in fact one of the few bright spots in Russ's life. Ever since Rachel had leased the extravagant apartment behind his back and he had forced on her a very tight spending policy, their marriage had been deteriorating.

"You didn't marry me for me, Rachel," he told her one evening when he came home. "My idea of a happy marriage is two people who love each other and work together for mutual fulfillment. Your idea of a happy marriage is this expensive apartment, wearing fancy clothes, and having a rich husband."

"Russ, that's not so. I wanted this apartment for Jamie."

Russ snorted. "For all Jamie knows, he could be living in a giant cardboard box. I'm sick of your pretensions, Rachel."

She looked at him pleadingly. "Are you sick of Jamie as well?"

He tensed. "What's that supposed to mean?"

"If you aren't willing to make our marriage work for my sake, Russ, aren't you at least willing to do it for Jamie's?"

"All right. Yes. I am."

For Jamie's sake he did try. But Rachel didn't make it easy, continuing to voice her disapproval of the clinic. One night when he was there working late alone, trying to diagnose an illness one of his patients suffered from, she turned up wanting him to take her to a movie.

"I can't do it, Rachel. I've got to work."

"You've been working late every night the past week!" she pouted.

"I know. And maybe I'll be doing the same next

week as well. I've got to do it until I can figure out what Mr. Oliver's problem is."

She slapped her hand down sharply on his desk. "Meanwhile, what am I supposed to do? You don't have any time for me or even for Jamie. It's clinic, clinic, clinic. If you were at least making some money for all the time you spend here, maybe I could understand, but you don't and you never will. There's no money to buy anything or to do anything special. Is this how the rest of our life is going to be?"

"Very likely it is," he said brusquely. "Now if you'll excuse me, I've got to get back to work."

She slammed the door when she left.

A couple of hours later, the source of Mr. Oliver's illness still eluding him, Russ locked up and headed home, then, changing his mind, went to his parents' house to talk to Alice instead. It was Jim and Mary's bridge night and they wouldn't be home.

She made coffee for them, and they sat at the kitchen table drinking it. "You look discouraged," she said.

"I am discouraged."

"Is it Mr. Oliver?"

"Some. But mostly it's Rachel. I've about had it with her, and the marriage as well, Jamie or no Jamie." He told her about their fight tonight at the clinic, then said, "It's funny. Except for the very beginning, we've had only one really happy period in our whole marriage. It was when Rachel came back after leaving me to live with her mother. Everything was fine or seemed to be. She was even eager to have a baby. Remember how I told you she insisted on the pregnancy test before she'd scarcely had a chance to get pregnant?"

Alice took a swallow of coffee. "But she could have

gotten pregnant before she left you."

Russ got up to pour himself a second cup. "No, she couldn't have. We'd been having a rotten time before she left. She wouldn't let me come anywhere near her—and hadn't for weeks." He returned to the table to see Alice staring up at him, the color draining out of her face. "What is it, Alice? What's wrong?"

Before she could answer, he heard his father's car in the drive, and shortly after, his parents walked into the house. Before either of them could say anything, Alice said, "You got home just in time to tell Russ good night. He was about to leave."

He hadn't had any intention of leaving, and still didn't know what had upset his sister, but she obviously didn't want to talk about it in front of Jim and Mary. Maybe he had upset her with all his talk of marital discord. So he said good night and went home.

After Steven regained his memory—and apologized profusely to Alice for the anguish he had put her through—and after he was back on his feet, he and Alice started dating again. Alice's mother didn't much approve, sure that Alice would be hurt again. But her father felt that Alice's decisions were hers alone to make, and if she loved Steven and wanted to be with him, well, so be it.

The day after Russ's revelation, Alice kept reaching for the phone to call Steven and break the dinner date she had with him that night. But finally she decided to go ahead and keep the date. She would tell him then what had to be told.

She met him at the door and sat with him on the porch swing. "We have something to talk about, Steven."

He frowned. "What is it? Is it about how you feel about me? Have you stopped loving me?"

"No." She bit her lip.

"Is it your parents? Do they object to our dating?"

When she shook her head, he began again, "Do you still want to see me, Alice? Do you still want us to try to be like we were before?"

She buried her face in her hands. "Steven, please stop asking me all these questions."

Taking her hands from her face and looking at her with grave concern, he said, "Alice, what is it?"

Then she told him.

"I simply didn't believe her," Steve said, his face paling. "I thought she was only trying to make me think I was the father. But if Russ says . . ." He turned and looked at Alice imploringly.

She nodded. "Then you *are* Jamie's father. When you wouldn't believe her and do something about it, she returned to Russ and passed Jamie off as his child."

"But why—if she decided to deceive Russ—why did she tell you the truth?"

Alice gave a little shake of her head. "Do you really have to ask me that? She told me because she wanted to wreck our lives, yours and mine. If she couldn't have you, she wasn't about to let me have you either."

"She's insane," Steven said.

Alice gave that same little shake of her head. "No. Not insane, Steven. Just incredibly selfish." She was silent for a bit. "There's Russ to think about now. The only reason he's staying with Rachel at this point is Jamie. Somebody has to tell him Jamie isn't his son, that he's yours."

The somebody was Jim Matthews, who volunteered that night after Alice talked to her parents. The next morning, when Russ came by to have breakfast with them—something he'd gotten into the habit of doing as his marriage began to deteriorate—his father broke the news.

Instead of going from his parents' house to the clinic, he went back to the fancy apartment, where Rachel was making a half-hearted attempt to clean the living room.

She looked up in surprise at seeing him. When he coldly told her to sit down because he had something to say to her, her eyes widened in fright. "What is it?" she asked. "Why are you acting like this?"

"You haven't any idea?"

"No. None at all."

Russ's eyes flashed in anger. "You're a liar, Rachel. You've always been a liar and a cheat. I've known that for a long time, but for Jamie's sake I tried to close my eyes to it, and now I've found out he's the biggest lie, the biggest cheat of all. How could you do it, Rachel? How could you be so low as to pass Jamie off to me as my son when you've known from the beginning he was Steve Frame's child?"

"That's ridiculous," Rachel said. "How can you say that?"

"It's not ridiculous. It's true. When you met me, you thought I came from a wealthy family, and so you went after me. Then when you found out I didn't have money and Steve came along, you went after him. It didn't matter that he was already taken. You threw yourself at him. Then, when you got pregnant and he wanted nothing to do with you, you came back to me because you didn't have anywhere else to go."

Rachel had never been one to give up easily, and she put up a struggle now. "Russ," she said, "I came back to you because I love you."

But Rachel had lost whatever power she once held

over Russ. He turned to her, his eyes like ice, and said, "There's only one person you've every loved, Rachel, and that's yourself. You even used your own baby as a means of getting us into an apartment I'd already told you I couldn't afford. Well, you can have it all to yourself now, Rachel, because I'm leaving you. We're through."

And with that, he walked out of the living room into their bedroom, packed his clothes, and left.

Chapter Five
Affairs of the Heart

The next day, when Steve called Rachel to say he wanted to talk to her about Jamie, she jumped to the conclusion that the only thing standing between her and marriage to Steve was her marriage to Russ. Since that was over, she could get a divorce and marry Steve.

When he came to her apartment at the appointed hour, six-thirty that evening, she was dressed up in a royal blue silk skirt and blouse, her hair washed and brushed, her mascara carefully applied, her lips glistening pink. She took Steve into the bedroom to admire his sleeping son, then led him back into the living room to sit on the sofa. "I'm so glad you're here," she said, sitting beside him. "I've waited a long time for this."

"Rachel," he said edging away from her, "I came here to talk to you about Jamie."

"Yes, I know that," she agreed. "But about us too." Again she moved beside him. "I know you love me, Steve, and you want to marry me. So as soon as I get my divorce from Russ, I'll . . ."

"Wait a minute." Steve stood abruptly and moved

across the room. "You've got the wrong idea, Rachel. I came here only to talk about Jamie. I accept the fact that he's my child, and I'm willing to pay child support. I'm even willing to pay for you to stay in this apartment, if that's what you want."

"But Steve," she cried, bewildered, "what I want is love. What I want is marriage."

"That may be, but you're not getting it from me. I have no intention of marrying you, Rachel, now or ever. I love Alice. I always have. She's the only woman I've ever wanted to live with."

Rachel made a face. "Alice? That little piece of fluff?"

Steve's face began to darken. "Cut it out, Rachel. Get this through your head. It's Alice I love. But even if she never marries me, I'll never marry you. Is that clear?"

"I always thought you loved me," she said haltingly.

"I didn't, and I don't. I'll have my lawyer work out a money settlement for you. I owe that to you and to Jamie. But I want to make one thing very clear. In the future I want nothing—absolutely nothing—to do with you." With that, he went out, leaving behind him an incredulous Rachel, a Rachel still determined to have him.

Rachel's version of the confrontation was that Alice had poisoned Steve's mind against her. She told this to her mother, and even tried telling it to Alice when she ran into her a few days later at Russ's clinic. "You always hated me from the very beginning," she said. "You were jealous of me because Steve loved me more than he loved you, and now you've told Russ about Steve and me to break up our marriage and leave Jamie without a father."

"I didn't tell Russ," Alice said coolly. "My father did. Frankly, I'm glad he did because now Russ is through with you. Now he knows what I've known all along, that you're a scheming, selfish, lying cheat, who's finally gotten exactly what she deserves."

One sad result of these troubles was Alice's decision to leave Bay City. Rachel didn't even get the satisfaction of saying it was she who had driven Alice away, for it was an argument between Russ and Steve that was the final blow.

Steve was more than willing to take the blame for his one-night stand with Rachel, but even that admission wasn't enough to dissipate the bitterness Russ harbored against him. "Rachel is a child," Russ said angrily one night, in Alice's presence. "Emotionally at least. And she's not very bright. You're a man, a mature, responsible man. Couldn't you have seen what the consequences were going to be for all of us? Or didn't you care?"

"Of course I cared, Russ," Steve protested. "I cared very much—"

It was useless. "As far as I'm concerned," Russ said, as if Steve hadn't spoken, "the only good thing to come out of this whole mess was Alice's breaking her engagement to you. She found out exactly what kind of person you are. I wouldn't blame her if she never had anything more to do with you."

After Russ had time to cool down, aware that Alice and Steve still loved each other, he apologized to his sister, but Alice felt she had to get away—from Steven, from her family, from Bay City—to try to put things in perspective, sort out her life, decide what she wanted to do. And most of all, decide whether or not Steven Frame was going to play a part in it.

"May I write you?" he asked her.

"Maybe, Steven. I don't know."

"Will you even let me know where you are?"

"I don't know where I'll be myself." She was talking of going to Europe—to England and maybe then to France. "Anyhow, the whole point of this is to give me a chance to think. If I get letters from you, it will be the same as if I'd stayed in Bay City."

"All right," he said. "I understand. But I hope you'll send a postcard now and then just to let me know how you are."

"I'd rather not make promises," she said.

He gave her a friendship ring. It was an old-fashioned gold band, wide and etched with flowers. He said softly, "I wanted you to have something to remind you of me."

Her blue eyes filled with tears. "Do you really think I need this to remember you? Don't you think I'm going to be thinking of you too much as it is?"

"I love you, Alice."

The tears ran down her face. "I love you too."

He had come to her parents' house to say good-bye. Now he said, "I'm not going to say good-bye because it can't be good-bye. I'll just say, 'Till I see you again.'" He kissed her and left.

The next day she flew to London.

Ever since his near-capitulation to Bernice on the day the twins were born, John had been steering clear of her. When he couldn't avoid seeing her, he made the meetings as brief and businesslike as possible. She made no protests—and no advances. Sometimes he felt she was laughing at him. Other times he felt she was playing with him, like a cat with a mouse.

During this period he tried several times to get Pat to

go out with him, to attend this or that party, accept this or that invitation, usually with no luck. He also urged her to consult her doctor, but she always put it off.

Alice had been gone about a week when John made another attempt to get Pat "out of the doldrums," as he put it. A revival of Rodgers and Hammerstein's *Oklahoma* was on nationwide tour and was playing in Bay City.

"Let's see it tonight," he urged her at breakfast that morning. "We can have dinner first, wherever you want to, and then see the show."

"Oh, darling, I can't," Pat said with a sigh.

He frowned. "Why not?"

"For one thing I don't have anything to wear."

"So buy something."

She sighed again. "You can't just go out and buy a dress at the last minute. It always has to have alterations of some kind."

"Then wear one you already have." He put a hand up to block any protests. "And don't tell me you don't have anything. You have a closet full of clothes."

She brushed at a wisp of her blond hair. "I suppose I do, but I don't feel up to wearing any of them."

He had no answer to that, so he gave up. But on impulse after he got to the office he called his mother-in-law and asked her to speak to Pat, and she did, that same morning. On the excuse of stopping by to see the twins, Mary tried, as she had tried before, to get her older daughter to consult her obstetrician. And as before, Pat demurred.

"He'll just prescribe pills, Mom, and that's no solution."

Then Mary asked quietly, "And how do you feel about driving your husband into the arms of another woman?"

Pat looked startled. "What other woman?"

"I don't know. There may not even be one—yet. All I'm saying, Pat, is if you go on being indifferent to John he may start looking elsewhere."

Pat looked at her hands. "Mother, John understands what I'm going through."

"I'm not saying he doesn't. But the more frustrated he gets, the less understanding he's going to be. As for what you're going through, you'd be finished with it if you'd do what all of us want you to do—see a doctor."

Meanwhile, John, at his office, got a phone call from Bernice. "What can I do for you?" he said in a businesslike way.

"Solve a problem, I hope," she answered in a most unbusinesslike fashion, her voice husky, intimate. "Shall I tell you what the problem is, John?"

"If I'm to solve it, you'll have to."

She laughed her throaty laugh. "Of course. How dense of me."

He found himself wondering what she was wearing.

"What happened," she went on, "is this. Last night as I was leaving the office Steve gave me a bunch of papers to drop by with you on my way in this morning, including some notes he's made regarding the money he wants to settle on Rachel for Jamie's upkeep and a trust fund for him, plus a personal allowance for Rachel. The problem is I sprained my ankle this morning while I was getting dressed, so I'm laid up at least for today and maybe the next few days as well. What I was wondering is—I mean, I don't want to ask you to put yourself out coming here for them, but could you maybe ask your secretary or somebody in the firm to do it for you? Would that be possible, John?"

Simply talking to her sent his pulse racing. He

swallowed and said, "Yes, Bernice, I'll send somebody over."

"Good. Come anytime. Good-bye, John."

"Good-bye, Bernice." He cradled the phone and sat thinking for a few minutes. Finally, he told his secretary that he had to step out of the office for a little while and to take all his calls for him.

All the way to Bernice's apartment he told himself what a fool he was being, that he wouldn't go anywhere near her, simply take the papers and get out.

When he rang her bell, she called out, "I'm coming. It takes me a little while to get there." Eventually, she opened the door and, seeing him, gave one of her most provocative smiles. "Why, John, what a nice surprise. Come in, come in."

"I can't stay, Bernice," he said entering the living room. It's prettiness and comfort surprised him, and he felt soothed by the beiges, light browns, and pale yellows.

"No, of course you can't," she said, hobbling back to the sofa. "Come sit beside me for a moment while I show you what I have for you." She arranged herself on the sofa, then patted the cushion beside her.

He sat down, reasoning that, after all, they couldn't confer sitting yards apart.

"Most of this concerns Jamie," Bernice said, handing him one sheaf of notes, her hand brushing against his, sending the now-familiar pulse of electricity through him. "And Rachel," she added, apparently unaffected. "Rachel may not be very happy these days, but Steve is making her financially secure for the rest of her life. That ought to be something."

John couldn't believe Bernice was indifferent to him. Yet what kind of elaborate game could she be playing? "I doubt that she'll appreciate it," he said, trying to sound as cool and correct as she. He looked at the sums of money Steve had recommended for Jamie's day-to-day care and for the trust fund he wanted to set up for him, then at the size of Rachel's personal allowance. All the time he was conscious of Bernice's gaze upon him. "He's being extremely generous."

Bernice shrugged. "That's the kind of person he is."

John nodded his assent, putting the notes in his breast pocket. Turning to her, he asked, "What else do you have for me?"

He expected her to hand him the other papers on her lap. To his surprise—though all things considered, it shouldn't have been—she took his hand in hers and said, "What else I have I've had for a long time, my friend," and she half-pulled him toward her.

That motion was all his frustrated passions needed. He gathered her into his arms and kissed her, his heart pounding as she responded. He had, he suddenly realized, been yearning for months to undress her, to see what lay beneath those inviting lines. Now he succumbed, and unbuttoning her blouse, pulling it off her white shoulders, he buried his face between those surging breasts her clothes had barely constrained. Then he picked her up in his arms and carried her into the bedroom, where he made love to her—something else he'd been yearning to do for months.

Although everyone in Bay City who knew Rachel knew she wanted Steven Frame to marry her, she maintained she didn't want a divorce from Russ. She was always careful to point out that he had walked out on her, she, of course, having done nothing to deserve abandonment. For his part, Russ wanted as little notoriety as possible, and he agreed to pay for the divorce, letting Rachel file for it. But when she demanded alimony, he drew the line. She certainly didn't deserve support, nor did she need it. Not only was Steven Frame paying for Jamie's upkeep and the rent of the high-priced apartment, he was giving her a very generous personal allowance as well.

When her lawyer asked her what possible basis did she have for demanding alimony, she stared at him in astonishment. "He owes it to me. I was his wife, wasn't I?" For Rachel that was reason enough.

But not money enough. While the divorce suit was pending, Jim and Mary Matthews went to court to recover their trust fund money. Since Russ was the fund's sole trustee, the suit was ostensibly against him. However, since he sided with his parents, he entered a plea of no contention. Their real opponent was Rachel. For her part, she was determined that nobody was going to take her baby's money away from him.

The basis of the Matthews's suit was fraud, but Rachel's lawyer argued that Rachel had told Alice Matthews well before Jamie's birth that his father was Steven Frame, and Jim admitted on the stand that Alice had repeated this news to him more than once. The judge ruled that no fraud had been committed.

Rachel's joy in keeping the Matthews trust fund was short-lived: Steve summoned her to his office and ordered her to return it.

"Return it?"she said, furious. "How dare you even suggest it? That's my baby's money."

"It's their money, Rachel. They put it in trust for their grandchild, which Jamie isn't."

"I don't care," she said. "The judge told me I could keep it and I'm going to."

"If you do," Steve countered, "then I'll cut off your personal allowance."

She exploded, "You can't do that!"

"Ask your lawyer whether I can or not."

Her lawyer agreed with Steve.

"But he signed an agreement giving me the money," Rachel said. "Can he simply take it away from me?"

"He can't take away Jamie's support, but yes, he can cut off your personal allowance. If we went to court we might—and the word is *might*—get a little of it restored. A little of it, Rachel, because no judge in the world would hold him to what he's paying you now. Look, be sensible. You don't need the Matthews's money and Jamie doesn't need it. If you return it, it might improve your chances of getting alimony."

Rachel brightened. As Ada had pointed out, "You mention money to Rachel, and she lights up like a Christmas tree." But in the end, she returned the trust fund only when her lawyer threatened to drop her as a client. So she gave it back, testifying in the subsequent divorce hearing that she was doing it out of the goodness of her heart. If the judge believed that, he was the only one who did.

Nevertheless, Rachel's lawyer was confident he would win his case for alimony. His confidence grew when he got the judge to rule that while adultery was relevant to the divorce, it did not affect the payment of alimony, and payment of alimony was what the defendent—Russ—was contesting, not the divorce.

Imagine Steven Frame's astonishment then when John Randolph called him to the stand and got him to admit under oath that he was Jamie's father.

"Your honor," Rachel's lawyer said, jumping to his feet, "you've already agreed that the issue of paternity is not relevant to the payment of alimony."

John turned to the judge. "It's not paternity per se that I'm getting at. I'm merely establishing it to elicit further information that I submit is relevant to the payment of alimony."

The judge nodded to John. "You may proceed."

John continued, establishing that Steve had set up a trust fund for the baby, that he was paying Jamie's daily upkeep, and that, in addition, he was paying Rachel a very generous living allowance. All this was set forth in a document signed by both parties, which he introduced as evidence.

"Now, Mr. Frame," John said, "the plaintiff has testified she voluntarily returned the trust fund to Jim and Mary Matthews. Is that true?"

"No, it is not."

"Did you have anything to do with it?"

"Yes, I told Rachel to return it. She refused. I demanded that she return it or I would cut off her personal allowance. She then returned it."

The divorce was granted without alimony.

Rachel still had one card up her sleeve, or so she believed. She had been after Steve to spend time with his son, saying it was important that Jamie know his father, and know his father cared for him beyond providing financial support.

Steve agreed, asking only for a couple of weeks to make arrangements at the office.

Scarcely able to believe her ears, Rachel beamed. "That's great, Steve. If you're too busy during the week, we can make it Saturday or Sunday. We can go for a drive in the country and . . ."

He cut her off. "I'm talking about seeing Jamie, Rachel, not you. When I see him it's going to be without you."

Delight changed to anger. "Do you think I'm going to let you take him without me there to look after him? You don't know how to take care of a baby, so either I go along or you can forget it."

There matters rested until Steve came up with the solution: he would come to Rachel's apartment to see Jamie, with Ada present to take care of her grandson.

"He doesn't want you to be here," Ada told Rachel when she arrived for the first afternoon of the new arrangement. "He wants you out of the apartment before he gets here, and he says you're not to come back until he's gone."

Rachel was dumbfounded at first, and then erupted with anger. "I won't go for that, not for a minute. What right does Steve have to tell me I can't come and go in my own apartment when I feel like it!"

"You might bear in mind he's paying the rent here."

"I don't care if he is or he isn't. He's not going to order me around."

Her mother shrugged. "It's your decision, Rachel. Either Steve visits Jamie on his terms, or he doesn't visit him at all."

"Oh, all right," she grumbled. "It'll be his terms—for now." Certainly she didn't intend for these terms to last. Steven Frame might think he was finished with her; she, however, was far from being finished with him.

Alice left Bay City for Europe in early June. Around the middle of August she wrote Steven to say she was living in Avignon, France, working at a children's hospital and living with a local family. She was feeling better, she said, and he was not to worry about her. She said nothing about wanting to see him, however, and as thrilled as he was to hear from her, he didn't want to force himself on her.

Then another exchange of letters gave him new hope. Russ had written to Alice apologizing for his bitter confrontation with Steve. If Steve and Alice still loved each other, he said, he didn't want to stand in their way. Or, as he told his parents, "Why should three of us be miserable?"

Alice replied, saying that she understood his bitterness, that Steven had hurt both of them. She still didn't know whether she would marry Steven, she continued, but she wanted to know how Russ would feel if she did.

Encouraged by these events, Steve cabled Alice to say he was flying to London on business and from there would fly to Avignon to see her.

They met at a little bistro where she often ate. With a navy blue cape over her nurse's uniform, she looked more than ever like a fragile Dresden doll. Taking her hand Steve said, "Are you glad to see me, Alice?"

Tears shimmered in her blue eyes. "Glad and sorry, Steven. You complicate my life."

He squeezed the hand he held. "For me it makes life simple. All I want is to be with you, nothing more, nothing less."

"Oh Steven," she said, the tears brimming over.

"I love you, Alice."

She pulled her hand away, then put it out again to take his hand in hers. "I love you too, Steve. I think of you. I dream of you."

"Come back with me, Alice." He leaned forward intently.

"No, Steven, I can't. I've made a life for myself here, for a while at least. I can't walk out on it. Can you understand that?"

"Yes, darling. I do. But come back soon?"

She nodded. "I think so."

He squeezed her hand again. "Then I'll be content with that for now. Darling, there's something else.

When you do come back to Bay City, I'll have a surprise for you."

"What kind of surprise?"

His eyes twinkled. "No hints. But I think you'll like it. At least I hope you will."

A few hours later he was flying across the Atlantic feeling lonelier than ever, but also feeling more hopeful than he had in months. And he was looking forward to completing his surprise for Alice—her dreamhouse.

Chapter Six
Shady Business

Cindy Clark was part of the reason for Russ's softened attitude toward Steve. He had started dating Cindy soon after the divorce was granted, either leaving the clinic with her, or meeting her somewhere for dinner.

One evening, after saying good night to Russ at the door, she found her brother, Ted, a handsome young man with an all-American look about him, in the living room, watching television.

"Hi, Cindy," he said, rising to greet her. "How was your date?"

"Fine, thanks. Russ is so nice, sometimes I'm afraid I'm just not good enough for him." She would never say so, but she felt ashamed of their home and their neighborhood, and had never invited Russ in. It was because they were so poor that she had gone to the clinic in the first place. She sighed and laid her purse on the nearest chair.

"Forget it!" Ted smiled. "You're good enough for the best of them! By the way—did you lose these?" He jangled a set of keys.

"Oh, Ted," she said, delighted, "that's wonderful. Where did you find them?"

"Right where you left them," he countered, holding out a brown leather purse to her. "They were in this purse you were carrying the other day."

"Oh," she groaned, "yes. How stupid of me." She shook her head. "To think I looked everywhere for them but there. Oh, Ted. You're a darling."

He wanted to tell her he was anything but that, but he held his tongue.

Shortly before the clinic opened, Ted had come back to Bay City after living in St. Louis for four years, working as a waiter in a restaurant there. What Cindy and her mother were ignorant of was Ted's sideline—selling drugs.

Though more a drifter than a criminal, he had drifted, unfortunately, into drug trafficking to pick up some extra spending money, drifting in a little deeper because he'd spent more than he had. But in the end, he'd had some frightening moments in St. Louis. He made up his mind to pay back all the money he owed, get out of the trafficking, and stay out. In his opinion, the best thing he could do would be to leave St. Louis, to literally get lost.

Back home, living with his sister and mother once again, he found a job as a waiter in Bay City's Fireside Inn, and thought he'd found a new life, too. But fate was never so kind. As he was leaving the Inn one night, beginning for the first time in years to feel secure, he was approached on the street by one of his old St. Louis customers. Unfortunately, the man had not come to inquire about Ted's health; he wanted amphetamines.

"You don't understand," Ted said. "I'm out of that business. That's all behind me."

"I suppose," the man hissed, "you know they're looking for you in St. Louis."

Ted's heart almost leaped into his throat. "They've got nothing on me," he blustered, but even he didn't believe that.

Neither did his former customer. "Do you want me to tell them where they can find you?" The man leaned forward aggressively.

"N-no," he stuttered, backing off.

"Then get me some uppers, man."

"Where? I don't have the sources I had in St. Louis."

The man shrugged. "That's your problem, Clark, not mine. I'm sure if you use your head you can come up with something."

Ted supposed he could too. In fact, an idea had already popped into his head, something he didn't want to think about.

"I'll meet you here Thursday night," the thug continued, tapping Ted's chest with his finger.

"No!" Ted exclaimed. "This is only Tuesday. That's not enough time. I can't possibly get what you want in forty-eight hours. You've got to give me at least until Friday."

The man shrugged again. "All right, Friday. But be here and don't be empty-handed." He strode quickly into the dark.

Ted's probable source—his only source—was the clinic where Cindy worked. That night when he got home he took Cindy's keys out of her purse and had a duplicate set made the next day. He was only going to steal a handful of amphetamines and only this one time.

The next night, he left the Fireside Inn and, using Cindy's keys, let himself into the darkened clinic. Locating the drug cabinet by the light from the street lamps outside, he was opening it when he heard Russ's voice call out, "Who's there?" and turned to see Russ standing in the doorway, squinting in the gloom.

His first thought was that Russ might recognize him, so on impulse, he ducked his head and aimed himself at Russ's midriff, sending him spinning back. But as Russ was going down he cracked his head on the edge of Cindy's desk, and once on the floor he lay there motionless.

Terrified, Ted crept to his side to check his pulse. It was beating, he was alive. But how badly hurt he was, Ted didn't know. He phoned an ambulance, and raced back to the supply cabinet, where he found the amphetamines. Then, picking up a chair, he smashed the window in the room to make the break-in look like an outside job. From a few blocks away came the high-pitched whine of the approaching siren. Telling himself he didn't have to lock up—an outside thief would have left by the front door—he slipped into the shadows beside the clinic and waited there, his heart pounding.

The ambulance arrived and still he waited, hating himself for what he had just done, praying that Russ would be all right. Only when the paramedics left the clinic carrying Russ on a stretcher did Ted slip away. He lingered outside his home until he was breathing normally and then went in.

Cindy was in the living room reading.

"Where's Mom?" Ted asked.

Cindy looked up and smiled. "She's gone upstairs to bed."

"Isn't that where you should be?" He could hardly bear to return her gaze.

"In a little while. I wanted to finish this."

Although Cindy's heart condition was a mild one, it

had the potential of becoming worse. She was supposed to avoid undue stress and strain. Ted didn't want to upset her, but he couldn't very well not tell her anything. She would know sooner or later.

"Cindy," he said, sitting down beside her on the couch, "I have a little bit of news for you."

"Oh?" she said, putting her book down, looking pleased. "What is it? Did you get a promotion at the restaurant?"

He shook his head. "No. It isn't that kind of news. It isn't good news at all. It isn't necessarily bad news," he hastened to add. "It's something I happened to see, and I figured you'd want me to tell you about it."

She was looking bewildered now. "What is it, Ted? What's happened?"

"I think maybe somebody broke into the clinic—"

"The clinic? Oh, Ted, what happened?" Bewilderment now gave way to alarm.

He put a hand on her arm. "Don't get upset. You know what the doctors say."

"Yes, I know, but I want to hear what happened. What makes you say somebody broke in?"

"Because when I was going past on my way home tonight an ambulance was pulling up. I figured somebody must have tried to break in, and somebody must have gotten hurt."

Cindy jumped to her feet. "It's Russ. Ted, I've got to get to the hospital!"

Ted stood up and grasped her shoulders, trying to calm her. "You don't know it's Russ."

"It has to be. He was working there alone tonight. Ted, I have to get to the hospital."

"All right. I'll take you there. But you have to calm down, Cindy, or you'll end up being a patient there yourself. Do you want that?"

"No."

"Then stay calm and I'll call a cab." He pointed to the sofa. "Sit."

She sat down.

"Do your breathing exercises."

She started doing them while he phoned for a cab.

Russ had had good instincts about Cindy. Though her background was very like Rachel's, the two women couldn't have been more different. While Rachel was scheming and dishonest, Cindy was open and loyal. During the fifteen-minute cab ride to the hospital, her only concern was Russ's well-being.

With Ted at her side, Cindy hurried to the admissions desk.

"Has Dr. Russell Matthews been brought in?" Ted inquired.

The clerk consulted her file. "Yes. Dr. Matthews is in the ICU."

"What floor is it on?" Cindy blurted out.

"The second, but you can't go up there."

The admissions clerk might as well have been speaking to the wind. Almost before the woman's words were out of her mouth, Cindy had grabbed Ted's hand and pulled him to the hospital's bank of elevators. A minute later they were at the door to the ICU. Jim and Mary Matthews were already there.

"Oh, Mrs. Matthews," Cindy implored, "is he going to be all right?"

Mary put an arm around her. "We don't know, Cindy. We're still waiting to hear."

"What happened to him? I mean, I know about the break-in. Or Ted thinks it was was a break-in—he saw the ambulance there. But what—how did Russ get hurt?"

"There must have been a scuffle," Jim Matthews

said, "and Russ struck his head against something sharp. That's what knocked him out. The neurosurgeon is with him."

No one could think of anything else to say, and only paced or fidgeted, now and again peering into the ICU, waiting for the neurosurgeon to come out. In about twenty minutes' time he did. "He's going to be all right," he said. "We won't have to operate. He's come around on his own."

"Thank God," Mary, Jim, and Cindy said in unison. Ted said nothing but thanked God silently, for helping him out one more time. He was absolutely determined that whatever threats his old customers made against him, he would move far far away from St. Louis, or Bay City, or the end of the Earth, before he would ever again steal anything.

When he got off from work Friday night, Ted went outside to meet his customer, and waited over an hour for him, but the man never showed. Thinking something had happened to prevent his meeting Friday night, Ted waited again on Saturday, but in vain.

For the next several nights Ted left the Fireside Inn expecting the man to be hovering in the shadows, but he never was. Ted speculated that maybe he was dead—killed in an encounter with another drug dealer. Not wanting to be caught with the amphetamines on him, Ted flushed them down the toilet and tried to forget the incident.

The pity was he forgot the duplicate keys.

Standing at her bedroom window after their first passionate lovemaking, wrapped in a black satin robe, Bernice watched John Randolph leave the building and get into his car for the drive back to his office.

Smiling, she turned back to her side of her rumpled bed and unwound the tape from her ankle. The ruse had worked, as she had expected it to. The next few weeks were going to be very gratifying; maybe even the next few months—about as far ahead as she ever looked.

Indeed, her prediction was correct. Though John told himself there would be no more repeats of that summer morning, he knew he didn't mean it. Far from satisfying him, his encounter with her had only inflamed his passion. He could hardly wait to see her again. From spending a good deal of time and energy trying to interest his wife in going places, John suddenly had no time himself for going out. More evenings than not, he was "working late at the office."

In the beginning Pat didn't care. She almost didn't notice. But one day toward the end of August two things happened that brought her up short.

The first concerned the twins, Michael and Marianne. The Randolphs' nursemaid, Caroline, usually brought the twins to their mother for what she called "together time" in the middle of the morning and again after the babies' afternoon nap. This particular afternoon both twins started fretting as soon as Caroline put them down. It seemed like neither of them wanted to have anything to do with their own mother.

Caroline tried to brush it off, saying, "They didn't sleep well last night, Mrs. Randolph. I'm sure that's all it is."

"Yes," Pat said, "I'm sure it is, too," but she was hurt, and after Caroline had made several unsuccessful attempts to settle them down with their mother, Pat said, "You might as well take them back to the nursery, Caroline."

When they were gone, Pat sat alone in the living room, depressed, discouraged, full of self-pity, thinking about the times her own mother and her husband, too, had urged her to see the obstetrician about her continuing depression. Thinking that maybe the time had come to consult him, she decided first to speak to John and ask him to go with her.

His secretary answered her call. "I'm sorry, Mrs. Randolph, but he isn't here."

"Can you tell me where he is?" *He's probably with Steven Frame*, she said to herself reassuringly.

"No, I'm sorry, but I can't. I don't know where he is. All he said was, he was going out for a little while and to take any calls that came in for him. Shall I have him call you when he gets back?"

"Yes, please."

Pat hung up the phone, puzzled. It was unlike John to go off that way in the middle of the afternoon and not say where. Something unexpected must have come up.

With a sigh, she forced herself to call the obstetrician's office and made an appointment for the following Tuesday.

When John got back to her he sounded anxious. "Is everything all right, Pat?"

"Yes," she said. "Where were you?"

"I was with a client."

He offered no more than that and she didn't inquire. He had always been close-mouthed about his clients. She took a deep breath. "I'm seeing the doctor next week."

"Well, that's great, Pat."

Having intended to ask him to go with her, she now found herself afraid he would say he didn't have the time for it, and that would make her feel foolish. And then, he might say of course he'd go with her, but that would make her feel childish. She decided to ask her mother to go instead.

As he had been so many nights recently, John was late getting home that night.

"You must have a spate of new clients," Pat said, fixing a drink for each of them.

"Not so many new ones. Just old ones with a lot of new work." John slumped into his armchair. "Wow, honey, this drink is strong."

"Oh? Sorry. Well, have a couple of swallows and then water it down."

He set his glass on a side table. "I think I'll let it water itself down while I go have a peek at my two favorite children. Coming?"

Pat put her own drink down and followed him to the nursery. Caroline had just finished giving them their supper, and they greeted their father with gurgles of delight, which, much as she tried to deny it to herself, further irritated Pat. She slipped away and went back downstairs to her drink.

Dinner had become a more or less silent affair, and tonight was no different. John was wrapped up in thoughts of his own, Pat in her usual state of depression. And after dinner he seemed to have more work to do.

"Honey," Pat ventured, "you've been working later and later at the office, do you have to work at home too?" He only smiled apologetically and went back to his papers.

The following Tuesday, her mother with her, Pat went to see her obstetrician.

"You should have come to see me before this," he said.

"Yes, I know. I kept thinking the depression would go away on its own."

The doctor reached for his prescription pad and scribbled something. "We'll give it a helping hand," he said cheerfully.

She and her mother went to a downtown pharmacy to have it filled, then to a restaurant for a cup of tea, where Pat took her first tablet.

Taking them three times a day, she felt noticeably better by the end of the week, and on Sunday afternoon she went to a football game with John.

"Oh, John! That was so much fun!" she said on the way home from the game. "It's so good to be feeling better, do you think we could go out for dinner and a movie tomorrow night?"

"I don't know if I'll be able to, Pat," he said vaguely. "I'll have to take a look at my schedule when I get to the office tomorrow morning. I'll call you and let you know."

The next morning he called to say he was sorry, but he wouldn't be able to get away in time. Maybe they could do something later in the week.

Later in the week proved to be as elusive as the Monday night dinner and movie.

The following Monday night, John called to say he had to stay late at the office again. Pat, deciding to pass by on her way to the downtown shopping mall, chanced to look up at his office. The windows were dark. Not believing her own eyes, she parked the car, went into the building, and took the elevator up to the floor his office was on.

Though there were lights on in other offices, John's suite of offices was dark. She began to feel terribly uneasy, but told herself he must have left just before she got there. Still, she couldn't shake her anxiety, and instead of going shopping, she drove home. However, he wasn't there and didn't arrive until almost an hour later.

"A hard day, darling?" she asked, fixing them both a drink, remembering to give him the weaker one.

"Pretty hard," he said.

"Isn't it kind of lonely working in the office when everybody else has gone?"

"A little, yes," he said, and her heart sank. "But the building has a night security staff, so it's not too bad. How are the twins?"

"Asleep. Caroline put them down over an hour ago. They miss seeing you."

"I'll try and do better tomorrow."

Pat decided she would do better tomorrow herself.

The next afternoon around four-thirty, she drove her car downtown and parked on a side street that gave her a view of the entrance to John's law office building. Feeling a little embarrassed, telling herself there was probably a perfectly ordinary explanation to John's whereabouts last night, nevertheless she sat in her car and waited for him to come out.

Shortly after five he emerged and headed for the garage. In a few minutes she saw him pull out and turn left. Starting up her own engine, she followed him.

She nearly lost him a couple of times in the rush-hour traffic, but managed to keep him in sight. Where can he be going? she wondered; then she realized he was heading for Steven Frame Enterprises. He had to be.

John pulled into the private parking lot that Steve kept for his employees, where he parked his car, got out, and went into the building.

Pat parked across the street, and rested her hands on the steering wheel. What could she say if John spotted her? She pondered this restlessly and couldn't come up with any legitimate reasons.

Finally, aware that he sometimes worked in Steve's

office and, thoroughly ashamed of herself for having doubted him, she turned on the ignition of her car, ready to pull away, when she saw him come out of Steve's building with Bernice Kline.

Knowing that John often worked with Bernice, either in his own office or at Steve's, she reasoned that maybe he and Bernice were just happening to leave together.

She was a little more alarmed when the two of them headed for his car, but maybe Bernice's car was in the garage being repaired, and John had offered to drive her home. It would be like him to do that.

But a shock of fear ran through her, and she had no answer at all for what happened when John and Bernice got into his car, for she turned to him and he to her, and then they were in each other's arms as though this was what they'd been waiting all day for.

Probably, Pat told herself, *they've been waiting for it ever since John left her the night before.*

She watched them move reluctantly apart, John started his car, and pulled out of the parking lot into the pulsing flow of traffic.

Pat sat where she was for some time, feeling faint and distraught. She recalled her mother's warnings those few weeks earlier. Couldn't she herself be partly responsible? At last, she started the car and drove home.

Caroline was just giving the twins their supper. "Well," she said brightly to the twins, "there's your mama. How about that?"

This time, their little faces smeared with porridge, they chortled and cooed with delight at the sight of her. She fought off her tears and put on a happy face instead, helping Caroline feed them.

"I'll put them to bed tonight," she told Caroline, thanking her.

"They'll be sorry to miss their daddy," Caroline said. "I suppose he's working late again."

"Yes," Pat said, "he is."

She felt empty and restless as she went back downstairs. Fixing herself a drink, she sat on the sofa in the half-dark, trying to think what to do. *I know Bernice seduced him,* she told herself. *Maybe I could do that too.* Then she got up and fixed herself a second drink.

Two drinks were all she intended to have. One was all the doctor would have approved of, and a weak one at that.

The doctor. She remembered the little bottle of pills in the medicine cabinet. But when she finally got up from the sofa, it was only to fix herself another drink.

Chapter Seven
Finding a Husband

Coming home from the hospital the night Russ was injured, Mary and Jim Matthews called Pat and John to tell them what had happened and that Russ was going to be all right. Next, they called Alice in Avignon to give her the same news.

Alice was distraught. "Do you think I should come home, Mom?"

"No, darling. At least not on Russ's account. If you're ready to come home yourself . . ."

"No, Mom, not yet. But soon, I think."

Her father spoke into the extension, "That's good to hear, darling."

"Dad," Alice said, "is Mom telling me the truth about Russ? Is he really all right?"

"Well, not this minute he isn't, no, but the doctor assured us he is going to be. He was conscious when we left the hospital. They're keeping him in Intensive Care for the first twenty-four hours to make sure he's stable, but they expect to move him to an ordinary room the day after tomorrow."

Alice sighed with relief. "I'll call him in a couple of days," she said. "When he's out of the ICU."

"Yes, do that," her mother and father chorused. "He'd love to hear from you," Mary added.

Alice and Russ had always been especially close. Alice, following Russ's lead, had gone into medicine, and it had been a treat for her to work with him at Bay City Memorial during his residency. When he had finished and opened the low-fee clinic with Dan Shearer, she missed him, and now that she was a couple of thousand miles away from him, she missed him even more.

"Are you really all right?" she asked anxiously when the overseas operator finally made their connection.

"I'm fine," he said.

"What about your head?"

"It's mending. I was only out a couple of minutes, Alice."

"A couple of minutes I bet," she retorted, pretending to scold him. "At least you sound like your old self—I'm only sorry I'm not there to cater to your every whim."

He grinned into the phone. "I am my old self. And guess who is catering to my every whim."

"Cindy?"

"That's right. She's sitting right here next to me." He took her hand and squeezed it. "When they let me go home I may take her with me, though I suppose Mom will want to put in her two cents' worth."

Alice laughed. "It sounds to me like you're going to come out of this thoroughly spoiled."

He raised his eyes to Cindy's. "I hope so."

"Russ," Alice said, turning serious again, "do you have any idea who broke into the clinic?"

"No. None. The lights were off in the drug-supply

room. I saw the guy, but I have only a vague idea of his size—and no idea at all what he looks like. He came at me so fast, I'm not sure I would have seen him even if there'd been more light." At that moment Ted Clark appeared in the doorway to Russ's room.

"Oh, Russ—!" Alice said, horrified. "I hate to think . . ." Her voice trailed off.

"Well," Russ said, motioning Ted to come in, "I have a visitor. Cindy's brother."

"I'll get off the phone then," Alice said. "Russ, please take care."

"I will, Sis. You too. And thanks for calling." Russ handed Cindy the phone and she set it down. "Come on in, Ted. Pull up that chair over there. Just put that stuff anywhere."

Ted put the extra pillow and blanket on the room's other bed. "How do you feel, Russ?"

"Okay. Better than okay. Pretty good, in fact."

Ted leaned forward in his chair. "Does your head ache?"

"A little, yes."

Cindy turned a worried face to his. "You didn't tell me that," she admonished.

He reassured her with a little pat. "You didn't ask and it doesn't hurt all that much." Turning to her brother, he said, "I appreciate your coming by, Ted. Cindy tells me you saw some of what happened at the clinic."

Ted nodded, looking at his hands. "Yeah."

"I don't suppose you got a look at the guy who broke in there."

"No. The only people I saw were the paramedics." Ted shifted in his chair. "I wasn't even sure what had happened. I more or less . . . well, put two and two together."

Russ sighed. "You sure put it together right." He sighed again. "The one thing that keeps puzzling me is who called for the ambulance."

"It must have been the man who broke in," Cindy said.

"You keep saying that," Russ said, "but I find it hard to believe. The man smashes a window, breaks into the clinic, comes at me like a freight train, and damn near kills me—and then he turns Good Samaritan and calls for an ambulance?" He shook his head. "It doesn't make any sense."

"But who else was there?" Cindy asked.

"I don't know." He ran his hand through his hair. "That's what has me puzzled."

"Maybe," Ted said, shifting his position again, "it was another passer-by like me."

"Maybe," Russ agreed, "only if that were the case, wouldn't you think he or she would have stayed around until the ambulance got there?"

Cindy said, "Maybe he or she did."

"Then Ted would have seen him. Or her." Russ looked at Ted. "And you didn't see anybody, did you, Ted?"

"No. Nobody." He shook his head. "Only the paramedics. Like I said before." He fidgeted with his pants cuff and cleared his throat. "Have the police learned anything?"

"Not that I know of." Russ turned back to Cindy. "What did Dan say this morning?"

"Not much," she answered, "and nothing about the police. If they know something, they haven't told him. They did dust for fingerprints the next morning, but I don't know if they got any."

Ted listened uneasily. Had he touched anything? He tried to remember.

Russ shook his head. "I wouldn't think they would. With all the patients in and out of there, and with Dan's and my prints—and yours, too, Cindy—on everything, I would think all the police would get would be one big smudge after another."

Cindy smiled pensively. "That makes a funny picture."

"If not such a funny reality." Resigned, Russ leaned back into his pillows.

"Well," she said, "at least we're not going to have any more break-ins. Or we shouldn't anyhow. Dan did say to tell you that the locksmith is coming this afternoon to put in better locks and a burglar alarm system as well."

"Nothing like locking the barn after the horse has been stolen," he said ruefully.

Ted rose to his feet and walked toward the door. "I've got to be going."

"You just got here," Russ protested.

"I'll look in on you again, Russ." He put a hand up. "And don't bother seeing me out. I can find my own way."

Russ laughed. "Okay, Ted. Thanks again for stopping in."

Leaving Russ's room, Ted walked down the hall to the bank of elevators. As pleasant as it had been to be back home, it might not be a bad idea for him to move on to some other place, he thought, even if the police were to find *no* fingerprints. People were always talking about that restaurant over in Somerset—the Riverboat, wasn't it? Maybe he'd go there, see if there was a job for him. The owner ran a casino in the back room, or so the gossip went. A croupier would be a step up from a waiter. He would definitely go see what the prospects were.

* * *

Rachel, too, was embarking on a course of action that would take her again to the Riverboat. In a roundabout way, their paths would cross.

She had hired Brian Blake as her attorney, a tall, slender man, with movie-star looks. He had worked, first, for the retention of the trust fund, and then for alimony in her divorce from Russ. His suave manner and elegant clothes said money—and money always attracted Rachel.

As far as she knew, he was a bachelor with no attachments. One thing led to another—Rachel was a very attractive woman, after all—and soon they both had reason to recognize the advantage of Jamie's being too young to know what went on in his mother's bedroom.

All in all it was a nice arrangement. It would do until Steve Frame came to his senses, put the unattainable Alice Matthews behind him once and for all, and admitted to himself as well as to Rachel that she was the wife for him.

The ever-watchful Ada didn't know for certain that Rachel was having an affair with Brian Blake, but she did know that her daughter was, as she put it, chasing after him.

"You think he's going to marry you?" she asked skeptically. Rachel, fresh from the hairdresser, had brought Jamie over to spend the night because she and Brian were going to be out late.

Setting the baby down on the sofa, she patted at her hair and said, "Yes, as a matter of fact, I do."

"Has he asked you?"

"Not in so many words, Mom."

Ada snorted impatiently. "What other way is there except in so many words? A man doesn't ask a girl to marry him in sign language."

Choosing to ignore her mother's cynicism, she said primly, "Brian and I have a really deep understanding. He understands me and I understand him. Besides, he loves me."

Ada was thoroughly disgusted. "Has he said *that* in so many words?"

"Mom, I don't want to talk about it." It was Rachel's turn to huff.

"Well, I do. There's something about the way Brian Blake treats you that I don't like—like you were cheap, or something."

Outwardly, Rachel brushed aside her mother's warnings, but she decided that maybe she should pin Brian down. As they were undressing in her bedroom that night, she nestled against him, saying, "You know, I like you. I more than like you. I think you're the nicest, smartest, handsomest, and most exciting man I've ever known."

He leaned over and kissed her, then pulled back far enough to say, "More exciting than Steve Frame?"

Rachel shrugged away from him, slipped her dress over her head, bra strap falling down against her arm. "What's Steve got to do with it?"

"A good deal, I think." Brian loosened his tie and lay it on the dresser.

She turned and ran her hand over his chest, then unbuttoned his shirt, edging it over his fine, lean muscles and flung it over the chair behind him. "I don't really see Steve anymore," she said. "I don't see him the way I see you."

He pulled back once more to look at her. "Is that your choice or his?"

Rachel turned away from him again, confident he would follow. "What's the difference? What matters is how I feel about you. And how I feel about you is I wish we could be together all the time. Every moment."

He did follow her, running his hands the length of her slender form, and climbed into bed with her after undressing himself, but what he had to say—"I don't know about all the time, but we can certainly spend more time together"—wasn't what she'd hoped to hear. Nor did she make any progress as summer turned to fall, at least not in the form of a commitment.

When he went to New York City to see about joining a new law firm there, he took Rachel with him. She convinced herself that he would take the New York job and marry her. So certain was she, that she told Steve about it. "Brian wants to marry me," she said, "and I haven't made up my mind yet whether to or not. What do you think I should do, Steve?"

She was expecting to inflame Steve's jealousy. Instead he said, "If you want to marry him, fine."

Brian was in New York, alone this time—or so Rachel thought—for a follow-up. When he called that night and said that he missed her, she took it as an invitation to join him there. She was smiling smugly when he opened the door of his hotel room.

"Surprised?" she said brightly.

"What are you doing here?" he growled.

She was stunned. "I thought you'd be happy to see me."

"You thought. You've got a way of thinking all sorts of things. Why don't you ask once in a while? For your information, I've got all the company I need right now." Rachel could see a woman's coat and purse tossed on a chair.

"But you love me," she said inanely. "We're going to be married."

He shook his handsome head. "No, Rachel, I don't,

and no, we're not. I never told you I loved you or that I wanted to marry you. You dreamed that up all by yourself."

"But Brian . . ."

He was thoroughly disgusted. "You're a very attractive girl, and we've had a lot of good times together. But that's all it ever was—fun and games. I never wanted to marry you. I don't want to now, and I never will want to. Is that crystal clear?"

Humiliated and dejected, Rachel went back to Bay City the same night. When she told her mother what had happened, Ada said, "Didn't I tell you that you were in for this kind of letdown? Didn't I warn you? The trouble with you is you never listen to anybody but yourself, and you're always kidding yourself about how things are going to be."

Rachel tossed her pretty head defiantly. "I'll go to Somerset. My father will talk to me. He'll tell me what to do."

Ada shook her head. "Aren't you right back where you were before—building something up in your mind? You were so sure Brian Blake would be glad to see you in New York. Now you're just as sure your father is going to welcome you with open arms in Somerset. What if you're just as wrong about him as you were about Brian?"

As Ada predicted, Gerald Davis too felt she had brought the disaster with Brian on herself. And though he feigned sympathy, when Rachel announced that she was planning to spend a week with him, he turned her away.

"I'm sorry," he said, "but you've caught me at a bad time. I've got some people I have to meet, business people who are important to me. You'll just have to come and see me some other time."

She couldn't believe she had heard him right. "You mean you're not going to let me stay here with you?"

His patience was frayed. "Look, Rachel, there's something you've got to learn. Everybody has troubles, not just you. I've got troubles. I don't want to go into it, but I'm having a problem with my daughter right now."

Rachel was incredulous. "Your daughter? I'm your daughter!" she snapped.

"Oh. Well, yeah, you are. But I'm talking about Pammy, the daughter who grew up with me, and I've got to go deal with that problem now. If you want to have dinner here on me, fine. You do that. I'll see you around." He went back to his office and shut the door, leaving Rachel standing by the bar staring after him.

Ted Clark was sitting at the bar having a drink. He had spoken earlier to Gerald Davis about a job and had been turned down: There were no openings, the restaurateur told him. Now as he tried to think about what to do next, he saw Rachel walk over to a nearby table, sit down, and begin to cry.

Finally he went to her and said, "You don't have to tell me anything, but you're going to feel better if somebody's sitting with you." She didn't dispute that, so he pulled out a chair and sat down across from her. "Maybe the next thing you're going to do is ask me to get away from you. If you do, I'll go. But first I'd like to say I'm not trying to pick you up or anything. I know how you're feeling. I've been through it and I'd like to help."

She wiped her eyes and turned a bitter face to him. "How can you help me? You don't even know me."

"I know you're Mr. Davis's daughter. I also know you're feeling all alone."

Rachel was feeling more than all alone. She was

feeling the lowest she'd ever felt in her life. Telling her troubles to a sympathetic stranger seemed like a good idea. At least he wouldn't be critical like her mother or unfeeling like her father. "I don't know what to do or where to go," she said, dabbing at her eyes. "Everybody in Bay City thinks I've come here to spend a week with my father. How can I go home and say my father had no time for me?"

"Bay City's your home?" Ted said, surprised. "It's my home too."

"What are you doing here then?"

He shrugged. "I came to see your father too, about a job. He didn't have one."

"So are you going back to Bay City?"

He shrugged again. "I don't have to. I can stay here and be a friend to you—if that's what you want."

She drummed the table top with her slender fingers. "But you heard what my father said. I can't stay here."

"Not with him, no. But that doesn't mean you can't stay in Somerset. You can—we can both stay at a motel." He put up a hand. "No, don't get me wrong. I told you I wasn't trying to pick you up. You'll have your room, and I'll have mine. We can have dinner together in the evening if you like. We can spend time together during the day, for that matter. Whatever suits you."

Rachel half-expected this was another con job, but since she couldn't face returning to Bay City the very day she'd left it, she moved into a motel and was not surprised when Ted showed up that night for dinner. When he sided with her against her father, she said suspiciously, "Why are you being so nice to me?"

He walked with her to a table in the motel's dining room, and they sat down together. "I'm just a guy, Rachel. I'm nothing special. I work in the restaurant business, and I'm looking around for a restaurant of my own. I had one once, but I gave it up to come back to Bay City because that's where I wanted to be. I'm doubly glad now because you're there."

For the first time since meeting him she smiled. "I like hearing you say that. I was married to a man in Bay City, and his family didn't think I was good enough for their son."

"You're good enough for anyone's son."

Rachel liked hearing him say that too. She opened her purse and took out some pictures of Jamie. "That's our baby," she said, letting Ted assume she meant her husband's and her son. Why complicate things?

A waiter approached with menus, which they studied, then ordered dinner.

"I suppose," Ted said, "we ought to introduce ourselves. My name is Ted Clark."

"And mine is Rachel Matthews," Rachel said. "My husband was Russell Matthews. He's a doc—"

"I know Russ Matthews," Ted said, cutting her off. "My sister, Cindy, is engaged to him—or almost engaged to him. She's the receptionist at his clinic."

Now Rachel stared. "Well," she said. "What do you know about that?"

Ted frowned sympathetically. "Look, Rachel. We've found each other—sort of. And we're helping each other. Right?"

"You're helping me," she corrected him.

He nodded. "Yes. But by helping you I'm being helped too. If you know what I mean."

"I guess so. Yes."

"So why don't we wait and see what happens?"

"Why not?" she agreed. She lifted her napkin from the table and spread it carefully across her lap.

As the week progressed, Rachel and Ted spent more

and more time together. He wasn't sure how he was going to pay for his part of it, but he had some cash with him for incidentals, and everything else he put on his credit card. She insisted on paying her own way, and since she seemed to have plenty of money, he let her.

Toward the end of the week they were walking down the main street of town, pausing now and then to window shop. As they stood in front of a travel agency looking at the posters inviting them here, there, and everywhere, Rachel, turning to Ted, said, "I've been wanting to tell you how kind and thoughtful you've been to me. You didn't just listen. You gave me courage. No matter what happens to me from now on, I'll never forget these few days and how wonderful you were. You gave me the feeling you really cared for me."

"I did care, Rachel. And I do. The truth is I love you."

She looked down. "Ted, please don't say that unless you really mean it."

He moved closer, protectively, to her. "I do mean it, Rachel. I love you."

Now she was radiant, beaming a smile that lit up her very pretty heart-shaped face. "Oh, Ted. And I love you."

He took her hand in his. "Will you marry me, Rachel?"

"Yes, Ted. Yes."

Even more to Rachel's satisfaction than the knowledge that somebody loved her enough to want to marry her was the prospect of being given away by her father—a long-cherished dream. Gerald agreed to satisfy that longing at least, so Rachel and Ted were married in Somerset.

In Bay City, in the living room of their home, Mary

Matthews was saying to her husband, "I feel better about Alice and Steve now that Russ has Cindy. Maybe this means Rachel is out of the picture."

He shrugged. "Rachel's been out of the picture for a long time."

"Well, out of Russ's mind and heart, but—"

"But nothing," Jim cut in. "Rachel's out of Russ's life. Alice won't have to be reminded all the time of what Rachel did to him, and to her. Nobody will have to be."

The phone rang, and Mary hastened to answer it, but it was a wrong number. She turned away from the phone, disappointed. "I was hoping that was Pat."

"Why don't you call her?" Jim asked.

"I have. Either she's too busy to come to the phone, or she says she hasn't anything in particular to say."

Jim frowned. "I thought she was feeling better."

"She was for a while. But I think she's stopped taking her medication and doesn't want to admit it to me."

"Have you tried talking to John?"

Mary shook her head. "He's harder to get than Pat is. He spends more evenings at the office than he does at home."

Jim's frown deepened. "Do you think they're having problems?"

"Yes, but I don't know what kind, and I can't get Pat to admit anything is wrong."

"Maybe nothing is, darling. Perhaps it would be better not to interfere."

"I suppose," she said uncertainly.

"Is Pat still planning to give the engagement party for Russ and Cindy?"

"Yes."

"That might be what's keeping her occupied."

"Maybe," Mary said, but she looked and sounded as unconvinced as she felt.

While her parents were voicing their concern, Pat sat in her half-darkened living room nursing her fourth or fifth drink, wondering if John was with Bernice, sure he was, telling herself she had to pull herself together for Russ's party—and would after she had one more drink.

And in Steve Frame's bachelor apartment atop his private office, the phone rang. He went to answer it. "Steven Frame?" a male voice asked.

"Yes?"

"I have a cable for you. It reads as follows: 'Flying home tomorrow. Alice.'"

Chapter Eight
Wedding Bells

Alice hadn't said in her cable what time she was coming, but there was only one flight from New York, where she'd flown from Paris, and Steve was there to meet it. His heart contracted when he saw Alice come into the terminal.

"Alice," he said, embracing her. "How I love you."

She hugged him to her. "How I've waited to hear you say that."

He pulled back, searching her face intently. "Then you've come home to me?"

"Yes, Steven. I have."

He embraced her again.

They had collected her luggage, stowed it in his car, and were driving in from the airport along the bay, when he relayed the news he had for her. "It's Rachel, as you might have guessed by this time. She always manages to do something to hurt you, even though this time she says she's changed."

Alice turned in her seat to look at him. "What has she done now?"

"She's married Ted Clark, Cindy's brother."

The bay was on Alice's side of the car, a wind whipping up the water, sending it splashing onto the shore. They drove along in silence. Finally, Alice said, "So she's back in the family once again. Or will be when Russ marries Cindy."

Steve nodded. "That's right."

"How is she supposed to have changed?"

"She claims to be happy with Ted. Satisfied with him."

Alice looked at him quizzically. "Meaning she's no longer interested in you?"

"So I gathered from what she said."

"What exactly did she say?" Alice asked.

"She said she was sorry for all the trouble she's caused us and that it won't happen again."

Staring at a spot of dust on the dashboard, Alice digested that. "I find that hard to believe." She brushed the dust away with her finger.

"Yes, I do too. On the other hand, marriage is a pretty serious step to take, and God knows I've told her often enough that I want nothing to do with her now or ever."

"What's Ted Clark like?"

Steve shook his head. "I don't know. I suppose we'll have an opportunity to meet him at Russ and Cindy's engagement party. Maybe you can also get a bead on Rachel."

Alice nodded. "Maybe."

Steve put a hand on her knee. "But I don't want to talk about Rachel, darling. I want to talk about us."

Alice touched his hand. "You'll have to give me time to catch my breath, Steven."

He squeezed her knee before withdrawing his hand to the steering wheel. "That much and no more. Now that you've come home to me, my darling, I want us to get on with our lives."

But Rachel, whether she had changed or not, had another monkey wrench to throw their way.

She had married Ted letting him believe Russ was Jamie's father, but soon after their marriage she told him the truth. Ted then admitted he hadn't been a hundred percent honest either. While he had led her to believe he had some money, the truth was that all he had was his job as a waiter at the Fireside Inn. Even this seemed only temporary, because the owner of the restaurant was trying to sell it. Who knew what the new owner would do?

Once again Rachel went to see Steve at his office, telling him Ted's situation. "You could help Ted buy the restaurant, Steve," she urged.

By this time Rachel's gall had ceased to surprise him. Lacing his hands behind his head, he said, "Yes, I suppose I could, but why should I want to?"

"Don't you want your son to grow up in a stable environment?"

He saw her point and said so, adding that he knew nothing about the restaurant business. "Talk it over with your father, Rachel, and then get back to me."

Rachel's idea of talking it over with her father was to say to him, "Steve wants to go into the restaurant business with you as a coinvestor in the Fireside Inn. What do you think of that?"

"I don't know what I think about it. I'll have to look into it," Davis told her.

Going back to Steve, Rachel said, "My father thinks it's a wonderful idea, a really good investment. So he's helping Ted. Now what about you?"

Steve shook his head. "Rachel, hold on a minute. I can't even consider the idea until I've had a chance to look into it—with or without your father."

"I don't see what there is to look into," she retorted.

"The Fireside Inn, for one thing. And your husband, for another."

Rachel's dark eyes flashed. "But Ted's a wonderful person. He's smart, he works hard, he's honest, and he has great ideas about the restaurant business."

"That may be," Steve said. "But all I know about him is that he married you. Let me look into it and I'll get back to you."

He did look into it, and he talked it over with John Randolph. Rachel's argument about Jamie having a stable environment was a persuasive factor. But it also seemed to Steve that if Ted had a restaurant and did a good job with it, Rachel would also have a stable environment and a stable marriage. Maybe then she would stay out of his and Alice's lives. So after talking to Ted and looking into the restaurant, he agreed to lend Ted the money to buy it. All that remained, as far as he was concerned, was to find the right time and the right place to tell Alice.

But of course it was Rachel who told her.

Nobody wanted to see Rachel at Pat's party for Russ and Cindy, but as Alice explained to a friend, "How would Cindy feel if her own brother—whom she's very close to—wasn't invited to the engagement party? And Pat couldn't very well invite Ted and not invite Rachel."

A great many people were there, the party spilling out of the Randolph house onto the grounds around it. Pat hadn't entertained this big a crowd in a long time—in fact, she hadn't entertained much at all lately—and wasn't sure she could get through the strain of the evening. She passed through the crowd, playing hostess as best as she could remember, showing off the twins, urging people to the refreshments laid out on the dining-room table, a huge punch bowl as its centerpiece. And from time to time she ducked into the kitchen to have a little drink herself.

Alice, nervous about meeting Rachel, hoped to avoid her altogether, and Rachel, equally afraid that Alice would say something to embarrass or humiliate her, was equally tentative. However, they ran into each other on the terrace outside the living room. Rachel was with her new husband and introduced him to Alice, saying how happy they were together, that it had practically been love at first sight with them. Then she said, "I know I did some terrible things, Alice, and made a lot of trouble for you in the past, and I'm sorry for it. I really am."

Surprised and touched, Alice said, "That's a very nice thing for you to say, Rachel."

"I'm not just saying it. I mean it." She squeezed her husband's hand. "Ted and I really are happy."

Alice managed a smile. "I'm glad to hear that."

After a few more pleasantries, Alice excused herself and went back into the house. *Maybe Rachel has changed*, she thought to herself. *If so what a wonderful, miraculous thing that would be for all of us.*

They encountered one another again a short time later at the buffet in the dining room. Wanting to be as gracious as Rachel had been earlier, Alice said, "Ted seems very nice, Rachel."

She beamed. "He's not nice. He's wonderful. And Steve is wonderful too. So I hope things work out for you and him."

"Thank you, Rachel."

"I mean, I've always thought Steve was wonderful, and after what he did for us—for Ted and me—I think he's even more so," she rattled on effusively.

Alice knit her brows. "What did he do for you?"

"Why, he lent Ted the money to buy the Fireside Inn. But surely . . . I mean . . . you already knew that, didn't you?"

"No, I didn't."

At that moment Steve came up and Rachel fell all over herself apologizing for having blurted out information she thought Alice already knew. Steve, his face reddening with embarrassment and annoyance, tried to shut Rachel up. He managed to get Alice alone, and took her outside to the terrace.

"Alice, please listen—I've meant to tell you, only the time never seemed right—"

"What I don't understand," she said, "is why you hid it from me." Then before he could answer her she said, "No, I do understand. You knew I wouldn't approve of you helping them."

"Alice," he said, "that isn't it at all. If you'd just listen to me—"

She wouldn't. She turned and walked away from him, back into the house. A few minutes afterward, she left the party by herself and went home.

Had Alice stayed longer she would have seen that Pat was getting drunk. Her mother saw it right away; even Jim noticed.

"I can't understand it," Mary whispered to him.

Jim, ever the apologist for his children, said, "It's the strain she's under, darling, having this big a party for so many people." Even by this late hour the party had hardly thinned out at all. People were having too good a time, eating and drinking. Jim added, "She's overdone it trying to keep up with all her guests. Pat never did have much of a capacity for liquor."

"No," Mary agreed. "That's true."

"So don't worry about it. John will take care of it."

John did. Gripping an unsteady Pat firmly around the waist he managed to get her upstairs and into their bedroom, where she stretched out on the bed and almost immediately fell asleep.

John stood looking at her, then he went back downstairs, making excuses for her by saying that she seemed to have a touch of the flu.

Russ became concerned and wanted to go upstairs to have a look at her, but John pulled him aside, saying, "That's only a story I'm giving out. She had too much to drink and she's just upstairs sleeping."

"Oh," Russ said. "I'm sorry about that."

John shrugged, pretending to an indifference he didn't feel. "Once she's slept it off she'll be fine. She may have a hangover tomorrow morning, but so will a number of other folks here."

"I expect you're right."

"Where's Cindy?"

"She's waiting for me to bring her some food. Will you excuse me, John?"

"Yes. Of course."

Russ filled a plate for Cindy, then took it out to the terrace, where she sat on the glider. Handing her the plate, and sitting beside her, he said, "Are you okay?"

"Yes, Russ. Why do you ask?"

"You look tired."

"Well, I am a little tired. It's been an exciting evening."

He put his arm around her. "Maybe you've had too much excitement."

She turned a troubled face to him. "Darling, I'm not an invalid."

"No, but you don't take very good care of yourself either."

"I'll do better when we're married."

"You bet you will," he said, "because I'll be there to see that you do, like when it comes to eating." He pointed to the full plate she held on her lap.

She smiled apologetically. "I'm not really hungry or used to eating at this time of night."

"Here. I'll help you out." He took the plate and ate most of what was on it himself. Then, setting it aside, he put his arm around Cindy again. "Happy?"

"Very."

"Nice party?"

"Very."

"Do you love me?"

"You already know the answer to that. But I'll tell you again. Yes."

"How much?"

She put her arms around him and hugged him as tightly as she could. "That much."

He pulled away to smile at her. "I think you mean it. I really do." And he hugged her small body to him.

Russ didn't want Cindy to become overtired, so they left the party shortly afterward. Since they were the reason for the party, the remaining guests soon followed them. By midnight the last guest had gone. It was close to one o'clock before the caterers had finished cleaning up, but finally they too were gone, and John went upstairs to his and Pat's bedroom. He had supposed she would still be asleep, but she was awake, sitting on her side of the bed, still dressed in now-rumpled party clothes.

"Are you all right, darling?" John asked, concerned.

"I will be," she said. "Is the party over?"

"Yes. Everybody asked for you, wanting to tell you what a lovely party it was."

She had been sitting with her head down and raised it to look at him. "Did you tell them I was passed out?"

"No. I said you had a touch of the flu. Darling, I'm sorry, the party was too much for you."

She shrugged. "I'll be all right."

He sat down beside her and took her hand in both of his. "Will you?" he asked, more concerned than before. "It isn't like you to turn to alcohol for a crutch."

"No," she agreed, "it isn't, is it?" She withdrew her hand and got to her feet. "But then I don't have you to turn to, do I, since you spend all your free time with Bernice."

She looked directly at him, and for a few moments they stared at one another. Then Pat walked out of the bedroom, leaving John still sitting on the bed.

The morning after the party Cindy was helping her brother pack up his last belongings to take to Rachel's apartment, where he now lived as her husband. Two suitcases, a backpack, a shopping bag full of books, and other odds and ends were collected in the middle of his bedroom. "I think that does it," Ted said, surveying them.

"No, I think you're forgetting something," Cindy said, going out to the closet off the living room. She came back with his trench coat in her arms. "I think it'll go there on top of the books." She folded it, turning it upside down, and some keys fell out of a pocket. She picked them up to hand them to Ted, then looked at them, shocked. "These are the clinic keys."

"No," Ted said, holding out his hand. "They're some keys I had in St. Louis. Here, I'll take them."

But Cindy held on to them. "They're the clinic keys, Ted. I recognize them." She fingered them. "This one is the front-door key, or it was, before we had the locks changed. And this is the key to the drug cabinet." The color drained from her face. "I think," she said, her voice choked, "I have to sit down somewhere." She walked from his bedroom into the living room and sat down on the shabby sofa. In a few minutes Ted joined her. "Cindy," he said, standing in front of her, his voice cracking, "if I had known he was there, I wouldn't have gone in."

For a long time the room was silent. Finally, Cindy said, "My own brother. I can't believe it. My own brother." She turned an anguished face to him. "Ted, how could you?"

Ted knelt at her feet. "I was desperate. Cindy, listen. I can explain." He told her how he'd gotten mixed up in drug trafficking in St. Louis, how he'd got in over his head, how he'd made up his mind to get out of it. He then explained how he had come back to Bay City intending to stay clean and had done fine until this old customer turned up, demanding drugs, threatening him if he didn't come across. "Cindy, I swear to God I never would have gone in when I did, if I'd known Russ was there. You've got to believe me."

Still white-faced, Cindy nodded. "I do believe you, Ted."

He sat back on his haunches, an imploring look on his face. "What are you going to do?"

"I don't know."

Before she had finished speaking, he was on his knees to her again. "Do you have to do anything, Cindy? I mean, Russ is okay now and I'll pay for the damage. Cindy, please don't turn me in. I've finally got my life turned around. I know you wouldn't do this to me. They'll send me to jail, Cindy, and what would Rachel think of that? It would kill her that she was married to a common criminal. And what about Steve's investment in me? That would be money down

'd revoke my liquor license, and
restaurant would be finished. Cindy,
ou just forget about it?"

long time saying nothing, her face pale
ed's eyes never once left her face.

she said at last. "I won't turn you in. Go
r life, Ted."

dy." He rose to put his arms about her, but
aside and pushed him away.

n't, Ted, please. Don't." She got up, went to
oom, and closed the door.

vening she had a date with Russ. When he
pick her up, she was waiting for him on the
orch. He took one look at her and frowned.
's the matter, Cindy? Are you ill?"
o. Russ, I . . . I have to talk to you."
ll right." He sat down beside her on the porch
ng, taking her hand in his. "What is it? What do
a have to tell me?"

She swallowed and took her hand away. "I can't
marry you." She struggled with the diamond ring he
had given her, getting it off her finger finally. She
handed it to him. "I . . . I'm sorry, Russ."

He wouldn't take the ring. "Why can't you marry
me? What's happened?"

She wouldn't meet his eyes. "Nothing's happened. I
just don't think I'm right for you, Russ."

He had heard this from her more than once. "Don't
you think," he said gently, "I'm the judge of that?"

Tears gathered at the corners of her eyes and she put
her hands to her face.

"Cindy, last night you told me you loved me."

She nodded, unable to speak.

"Were you telling me the truth?"

She didn't answer.

"Cindy, I love you. I want to marry you."

She turned away from him abruptly, still unable answer.

"Cindy, something has happened, whether you willing to admit it or not. Can't you tell me what it Cindy, trust me. Please."

She struggled to get her feelings under contro clenching her hands, the diamond biting into he palm. Finally, she said, "Russ, don't make it an harder for me than it is. I can't marry you. I'm sorry Please go. Please."

He stood up. "All right. I'll go for now. But we're still engaged, Cindy. We're still getting married. We'll talk about it in the morning at the clinic."

The next morning Russ had an emergency house call to make. When he got to the clinic, there was a note on his desk from Cindy saying she was sorry, but she was resigning her receptionist job and returning his ring. Would he please forgive her? Beside the note lay the ring.

The morning after the party, when Alice told her parents at the breakfast table what Steven had done to cause their latest estrangement, her father, to her surprise, defended him. "He's a businessman," her father said. "He gets involved in all kinds of projects."

She scowled at him. "But why would he want to help Ted and Rachel?"

"Darling, now that Ted is Jamie's stepfather, Steve may feel he should help Ted get on his feet." Her father stirred sugar into his coffee. "I think there's something else you're overlooking."

Alice put her coffee cup down and glanced from her mother to her father. "What?"

Her mother kept quiet, leaving it to her husband to

explain. He did. "Has it occurred to you that Steve may have done this for you?" Jim asked.

Alice stared at him, confused. "For me?"

He nodded. "Yes. Darling, what's kept you and Steve apart all this time?"

Alice answered without hesitation. "Rachel." She picked up her cup and drank some of her coffee. "Everything has happened because of her being with him that night and getting pregnant with Jamie. But it's more than that. It's all the things she's done since, too."

"And," her mother put in, "it's the things she might do after you and Steven are married."

"That's right," Alice said. "I've worried and worried about how she would crowd Steven, the way she'd try to wheedle things from him."

"Yes," her father said. "Especially money. Are you beginning to see, Alice? By helping Ted buy the restaurant, Steve is giving him a chance to become financially independent. If Ted does that, then what excuse does Rachel have to come to Steve for money?"

Alice stared at her father in open-eyed wonder. Without another word, she went to the phone, called Steven, and apologized.

"Darling! I'm so glad you called! Let's celebrate with a picnic in the country." He couldn't hide his excitement.

"Where in the country?" Alice asked, intrigued.

"You'll see," he said. She could get nothing further from him.

When he picked her up at noon, he drove west of Bay City, in the direction of Somerset. About five miles out of the city, he turned off the highway onto an asphalt county road. A mile and a half further, he turned into a gravel drive. Alice saw a two-story, white-frame Colonial house set on beautifully landscaped and wooded grounds. Pulling up in the driveway, Steve stopped the car, got out, and came around to open Alice's door.

"Whose property is this?" she asked.

He smiled. "Would you believe me if I said it was yours?"

She stared at him. "Mine? Steven, I don't understand."

He gestured toward the house. "Do you like what you see?"

"Of course I do. It's the kind of house you and I have—" She broke off, clasping her hands. "Oh, Steven!"

His smile brightened. "It's the surprise I told you I was preparing for you, Alice. Your dreamhouse. You've seen the outside; now come on in!"

Taking Alice's hand, he led her into the house and through all the rooms. Upstairs were three bedrooms and a study for him. Downstairs there was a large, airy kitchen, a formal dining room, and a massive living room with floor-to-ceiling windows and a huge fireplace. Most of the rooms had floor-to-ceiling windows, all framing magnificent vistas of shrubs and flowers and grass and trees.

"Oh, Steven." By now she was breathless.

"And one more thing," he said. "Come back outside."

He led her to the rear of the house, to the broad flagstone terrace. Turning to her he said, "Will you marry me here, Alice?"

"Oh, darling," she said, looking from him to the terrace and back again to him, "yes, I will."

And so, after three weeks of frenzied preparation— the necessary finishing touches to invitations, trousseau shopping, showers, buying the twin gold bands, opening presents, and all the rest that goes into the planning of a big wedding—on September twenty-third, a day more like summer than fall, a beautiful, clear, bright day, Alice and Steven were married on the terrace in back of their dream-house. After the reception, they flew to St. Croix for an extended honeymoon.

That night, in the master bedroom of his vacation home, Steven Frame kissed his new bride tenderly. "Darling, you're the most important thing in the world to me. You always have been and you always will be."

"Oh, Steven," she answered, "I love you so."

She trembled slightly under the fluttering touch of his fingers as he caressed her shoulders.

"And I love you," he murmured.

Their tenderness turning to passion, clasped together on the nuptial bed, they consummated their love.

Meanwhile, that same night back in Bay City, a storm was brewing. Already, a fierce wind rattled the windows. Disturbed by it and her own thoughts, Rachel lay in bed unable to sleep.

She had told everybody that she and Ted were happy and very much in love, and even began to believe it herself. But the wedding today had changed all that.

She couldn't believe Steve had married Alice. All the old feelings came back: It wasn't fair, Alice didn't belong to Steve. *She* did. Steve only wanted Alice because she seemed so unattainable. It was Rachel he loved, Rachel who understood him, who knew what he wanted, Rachel who could truly make him happy.

One day I will, she vowed to herself. *Let Alice have*

her precious honeymoon, and then let Steve find out how little staying power Miss Dresden China Doll had.

Rachel got out of bed quietly so as not to wake Ted. She tiptoed down the hall to stand at Jamie's bedside, looking down at him. The night of his conception Rachel had discovered for the first time in her life what passion meant. She would have it again, she was sure.

One of these days, somehow or other, it would be her turn. Then Jamie would have a full-time father, and Rachel, not Alice, would be Mrs. Steven Frame.

Chapter Nine
A Christmas Gift

After Cindy left him her note, Russ made several attempts to see her, but without success. She always told her mother to say she was sorry but she couldn't talk to him. Then she would shut herself up in her bedroom and not come out again until Russ had gone.

Her mother worried about her. "You don't look well, honey. Shouldn't you see a doctor?"

"No, Mom. I'm okay." But she sounded almost as bad as she looked.

In the meantime, Ted was doing very well at the Fireside Inn. Customers increased daily as word spread through the community that, under its new management, the Fireside Inn was definitely worth a visit. But, as Ted soon discovered, running a restaurant is an exhausting, far from glamorous job. And Rachel was, as always, a very demanding wife. That left Ted little time to attend to his mother and sister, and he saw less and less of them as the weeks passed.

Russ went back to working long hours, trying to lose

himself in his work with the clinic and its patients. His parents worried about him, wondering, as he did, why Cindy had broken the engagement and quit her job. But they didn't have the same grounds for concern as Mrs. Clark. Finally she decided she must see her son and set off for the Fireside Inn to pay him a visit.

He led her to a table and sat down with her. It was about ten in the morning, and he wasn't as busy now as he would be in another hour or so.

"What is it, Mom?"

"It's Cindy. I'm worried about her, Ted."

He looked concerned. "Is she sick?"

"I think so, yes."

His frown deepened. "What do you mean, you think so?"

"She always denies anything is wrong, but you only have to look at her to know she's hiding something. Can you come see her?"

"Sure, Mom. Let me think a minute." He sat there, running through a mental list of chores and appointments. "How about three o' clock this afternoon?"

His mother brightened. "That would be wonderful, Ted."

"I won't be able to stay long."

"You won't have to."

When he arrived, he was appalled at how ill Cindy looked. "You have to go to a doctor, Sis."

She gave him a sad, despairing look. "It isn't a doctor I need, Ted," and would say no more.

Mrs. Clark didn't know what Cindy meant by that, but Ted did. Late that same night, after business at the Inn had slowed to a trickle, he called the clinic and was not surprised to find Russ there. "I have to see you," he said tersely.

"Come right away," Russ replied.

A few minutes later Russ opened the door and ushered him into his office, nodding to a chair. "What is it, Ted?"

"It's Cindy."

Alarmed, Russ said, "Is she all right?"

"She claims she is, but Mom and I don't think so. But that's only indirectly why I'm here." Taking a deep breath, he continued, "Russ, I'm the reason Cindy broke her engagement to you."

"You? What did you have to do with it?" he asked, puzzled.

"Everything." He told Russ of the break-in, of Cindy's discovery, and of his begging her not to turn him in. "If I'd known she was going to break off with you, I wouldn't have asked it of her. At least, I don't think I would have. But I can't stand it anymore, Russ. Please go to her."

Russ looked at his watch. "It's too late tonight, but I'll go there first thing in the morning." He contemplated Ted coolly. "What will you do?"

Ted shrugged. "The only thing I can do. I'm going home to tell Rachel, and then I'm going to turn myself in to the police." He tried a smile. "It's never too late to go to the precinct house. They're open around the clock."

Rachel was curled up on the sofa reading the paper when he got home. She was horrified, not so much by what he'd done as what he intended doing. "There's no reason for you to go to jail," she said. "I'll talk to Russ and get him not to press charges. It's the least he can do for me."

"Rachel," Ted said, when he could get a word in edgewise, "you don't understand. It's no longer in Russ's hands, if it ever was. It's a police matter."

"It isn't as long as they don't know about it. Ted, you can't do this." She threw the newspaper on the floor and paced the room.

He shook his head. "I have to do it. I've lived with it on my conscience long enough."

"But what about me and Jamie? Can't you think of anyone but yourself?"

"I'll work something out. Maybe I can get a suspended sentence."

Rachel did manage to talk to him out of turning himself in that night.

"You've waited this long," she reasoned. "You can wait a few hours longer. You need to get a lawyer first."

Ted was easily persuaded. "Yeah, I suppose you're right."

The next morning, Russ was at Cindy's house. He would not accept her refusal to see him. "Tell her," he said to Mrs. Clark, "that Ted came to see me last night to tell me why she broke our engagement."

Mrs. Clark went into Cindy's bedroom to deliver the message. A few minutes later, Cindy came out alone. Seeing how thin and pale she was, he took her in his arms. "The first thing we're going to do is get you to the clinic. I'm going to run some tests on you, young lady."

As he waited for her to get ready to go to the clinic with him, he fervently hoped that maybe all she needed was some tender loving care.

That same morning Ted hired a lawyer, then turned himself in to the police. For once, Russ felt as Rachel did, hoping that Ted wouldn't have to go to jail. Though he did, it was not for long. Taking all the extenuating circumstances into consideration, and after examining the various depositions testifying to the defendant's character, the judge sentenced him to thirty days in jail and three hundred and twenty hours of volunteer community work, to be performed over the next twelve months.

In order to protect the Fireside Inn's liquor license, a transfer of title had to be made to Rachel. The new owner maintained a facade of the devoted, stick-by-him wife, but privately she grumbled constantly about having to take on so much responsibility, not to mention the hard work involved. Now it was she who spent ten and twelve hours a day at the restaurant overseeing the deliveries, paying the staff, being gracious to the customers, listening to their complaints, even having to do some waitressing herself when somebody called in sick.

And every day, traveling back and forth from the apartment to the Inn, she passed a travel agency with tantalizing posters of the Caribbean displayed prominently in its windows. She couldn't help thinking about Steve and Alice on their honeymoon. *Having themselves a high old time, no doubt,* she fumed while she was stuck here in Bay City taking life's lumps as usual. Seeing those posters every day renewed her determination to take Steve away from Alice—and the sooner, the better.

Ever since the engagement party Pat had given for Russ and Cindy, and the subsequent bedroom revelations, John had been trying to break off with Bernice. They had never met daily, even in those first few heady weeks. But he had seen her as often as every other day before they had settled into meeting two or three times a week. Even so, this only seemed to leave him dissatisfied, wanting her more.

He tried to reach out to Pat, but she wouldn't let him

come near her. She no longer even slept in their bedroom but had moved to the guest room down the hall.

The illicit affair was affecting his work as well as his home life. A couple of times he had broken an appointment with a client to answer a telephoned summons from Bernice, the mere sound of her husky laugh enough to start desire coursing through him.

He told himself this was crazy, it had to stop, and said as much to Bernice.

They were lying in her bed when he said it, and had finished making love only minutes before. Bernice was lying face down beside him.

She put her hand on his bare chest. "Whatever you say, darling. I understand." She raised her sleek torso on her elbows and half-turned toward him, her tantilizing body stirring him again.

Mesmerized, he caressed her and knew as he did it that he was making a mistake, for in minutes they were making love again as passionately as if he had been denied her for a month.

Still, realizing that Pat's heavy drinking was a direct result of his affair, he was determined to break off with Bernice. Continuing this extramarital relationship was fair neither to his wife nor to the children, his two adored babies.

He was sure Pat had said nothing to her parents. If she had, he'd have heard about it. Every time the office phone rang he was torn between wanting it to be Bernice with another of her throaty summons and wanting it to be his father-in-law saying something had just come to his attention and would it be convenient if he stopped by John's office for a little talk.

Then, angry with himself, he would tell himself he

was a coward. Did he really need a conversation with his father-in-law to do the right thing for his marriage?

The question didn't need an answer, but this morning, before he had a chance to give it one, his secretary buzzed him to say that Bernice was on the phone.

Hoping against hope that this was a legitimate business call, he punched the lighted button on his phone and said, "Yes, Bernice, what I can I do for you?"

"I was hoping you could find some time in your schedule to stop by here this afternoon. There are some papers I have to send to Steve in St. Croix, but I'd like you to see them first."

John sighed both with relief and disappointment. Checking his desk calendar, he said, "How about three-thirty?"

"Three-thirty would be fine, John."

"Okay. See you then."

At three-thirty he was in Bernice's office. Having made up his mind before going that there would be no hanky-panky, he found that there was no opportunity for any. Bernice's secretary was with them the entire time.

Damn the woman, he thought, mopping his brow. She was being perfectly clear in her intentions: In denying John the opportunity to make a move toward her, in case he had that in mind, she was instilling in him a determination to find that opportunity somewhere else, and the sooner, the better.

Acting unaware of the struggle within him—another talent of hers—Bernice walked out of the office with him when they had finished.

"I need a breath of fresh air," she said as they walked together to the parking lot. Smiling her easy, catlike smile she added, "I also need the chance to be alone with you if only for a minute, darling."

The effect was the same as if she had touched him.

"I have to get back to my office, Bernice," he said uncomfortably. He fumbled for his car keys and pushed them into the lock.

She smiled again. "I know you do. I won't keep you. But how about coming to my apartment for dinner tonight? Just the two of us."

Was it impossible to say no to her? John steeled himself against the desire pulsating through his body. The time to think about what he was doing to his marriage and his family was not after making love to Bernice but before doing it. Before contemplating doing it. "No, Bernice," he said, surprising even himself, "I'm sorry but I can't. Not tonight."

As he expected, she didn't try to coax him out of his refusal. Bernice never asked twice, that was part of her strategy. She only smiled her catlike smile again, shrugged, and said, "Some other time then. Thanks for stopping by, John. I'll get the papers off to Steve today."

John drove back to his office half disappointed and half pleased with himself, feeling maybe he had turned a much-needed corner. Back in his own office he gave full attention to the work on his desk, and at five-thirty left the office for home.

When he pulled into the driveway, he was in better spirits than he had been in weeks. He found himself looking forward to spending some time with the twins and then the rest of the evening with his wife.

The living room was empty, and no sounds came from the kitchen. Supposing that Pat was up in the nursery with Caroline and the twins, anticipating his arrival there, he went upstairs to join them.

Caroline and the twins were in the nursery, but there was no sign of Pat. He said nothing, but played . with Michael and Marianne until it was time for Caroline to give them their supper. How much Caroline knew of their domestic difficulties John didn't know. He had never talked to her about it, and he doubted Pat did. He excused himself and went down the hall to the guest bedroom and knocked. There was no answer, so he opened the door and went in. The room reeked of whisky. Pat was sprawled in the easy chair, bottle in one hand, empty glass in the other. She turned her leaden gaze on him but didn't speak.

He didn't speak either. Filled with disgust and frightened by her silence, he retreated from the room and the sight of her, closing the door behind him. Then, from the phone in the kitchen, he called Bernice.

"What a nice surprise," she said smoothly, in response to his greeting.

"Is your dinner invitation still on?"

"If you'll give me thirty minutes."

"I can give you that."

"Wonderful. I'll see you later."

He spent the next half hour driving aimlessly around Bay City, in and out of the wharves that rimmed its downtown area, many of them rundown, sorry-looking mementoes of the days when ships were the kings of commerce.

He arrived at Bernice's apartment and fairly plunged into her arms, hardly noticing what she was wearing, so intent was he on taking it off her, and getting her into the bedroom.

Within minutes he was in bed with her, making love to her, devouring her with kisses and caresses, his passion thundering in his head and in his body until she, too, was carried away and they lay together quietly.

Alice and Steve returned from their honeymoon in late November. By that time Ted had served his thirty days in jail and was once again reunited with Rachel and Jamie. Best of all, from Rachel's standpoint, she was now freed from the Fireside Inn and its grueling demands. She continued as the restaurant's owner, but in name only, spending her days as she had before Ted went to jail, playing with Jamie, now almost three years old, gossiping with her mother, and doing what she liked best—shopping for clothes for herself and her child.

She was in Bryant's Department Store getting a start on her Christmas shopping when she spotted Alice with a woman friend. They were in the tearoom having coffee, a pile of packages on the chair between them. Rachel hung back, unseen by either of them, trying to figure out how she could approach them without being rebuffed.

Suddenly the friend glanced at her watch, uttered an exclamation of dismay, gathered her packages from the pile, kissed Alice's cheek, and hurried out of the tearoom right past Rachel, completely oblivious of her.

Rachel approached the table, smiling her self-effacing smile. "Hello, Alice. I heard you were back."

Alice had no smile for her. "Hello, Rachel. How are you?"

For Rachel that was invitation enough. Depositing her own packages on one of the vacant chairs, she pulled out the other one and sat down, ordered coffee from an approaching waitress, then turned back to Alice, saying pointedly, "We *are* letting the past be the past, aren't we, Alice? I mean, I know we can't exactly be friends, but we don't have to be enemies, do we?"

"No," Alice said, "we don't have to be enemies."

Rachel relaxed somewhat. "Oh, you don't know how much it means to me to hear you say that. I mean, with Steve being Jamie's father and all. I mean—well, you know what I mean."

"I guess so," Alice said.

Rachel smiled again and patted her long dark hair. "You don't know how pleased I am to run into you like this. I . . ." She dug in her purse for some snapshots and gave them to Alice. "I was going to mail these to Steve—they're some pictures of Jamie—go ahead, look at them—isn't he the handsomest little boy you've ever seen?"

Alice looked at the pictures. "He is handsome, Rachel."

Rachel beamed. "Doesn't he look just like his father?"

Alice looked at the pictures again. "I think he looks more like you."

"Well, like both of us, I guess. Anyhow, if you wouldn't mind giving them to Steve."

"No. Not at all." Alice put the snapshots in her purse.

"And if you wouldn't mind asking him something for me."

"Ask him what, Rachel?"

The waitress brought Rachel's coffee, and she busied herself stirring cream and sugar into it, taking so long Alice repeated her question. "Ask him what?"

"Well," Rachel said, "you see, Ted is around Jamie all the time. Since Ted and I are married—well, Jamie thinks Ted is his daddy. And I was wondering if you'd ask Steve if he'd let Jamie go on thinking that—I mean, until he's old enough so that we can explain it to him."

"Yes," Alice said, "I'll ask him."

Rachel exclaimed, relieved, "Oh, Alice, thanks. I really appreciate it. I mean, I'd ask him myself, but I never see Steve, not even when he comes to visit Jamie. But I guess you already know that—that Mom is there with Jamie when Steve comes to see him."

Alice nodded and finished her coffee. "Yes, I know. Now, Rachel, if you'll excuse my running out on you . . ."

Alice stood up and gathered her packages and her check. "Good-bye, Rachel. I'm sure that I'll see you around."

At the cashier's desk Alice paid her check, noticing as she did so that her hands were trembling. She shook her head, irritated. Less than fifteen minutes ago she had told her friend that she no longer worried about Rachel and her relationship, or lack of one, with Steven. And now after one encounter, she was shaking with fear.

She left the tearoom and the department store and went to get her car for the drive out to the dreamhouse she and Steven had come back to after their long, blissful honeymoon in St. Croix.

She couldn't imagine what Rachel was up to in giving her the snapshots and asking the favor, but she didn't doubt for a moment that she was up to something. For all Rachel's talk about having changed, Alice had yet to see any hard evidence of it. Surely Ted Clark's going to jail for attacking Russ and breaking into the clinic must have taken some of the bloom off their marriage.

Driving home she tried again to analyze Rachel's request, giving up finally. Maybe Rachel herself didn't know what she was up to, beyond keeping her hand in, so to speak. She was doing a splendid job of that.

Steven was home ahead of her, out of his office clothes, in jeans and a sweater, building a fire in the fireplace. He took her in his arms and kissed her. "How are you, my darling?"

Alice leaned back in his arms to smile at him. "Your darling is fine, and she'd be finer still if you'd sweep her off her poor, tired feet and take her upstairs and make love to her."

He laughed. "I was hoping you'd say that." And sweep her off her feet he did—and granted the rest of her request as well. Afterward, curled up beside him, she told him about seeing Rachel and the favor she wanted of Steve. "Why should I let my son think some other man is his father?" Steve asked.

"Maybe," Alice said, "for the same reason you lent Ted the money for the Fireside Inn. To keep Rachel's relationship to Ted stable."

Steve grunted. "You mean anything to keep her happy?"

"No. Not anything, and not if having Jamie know the truth is important to you."

"In some ways it is. I don't know, Alice. I'll have to think about it."

In the end he agreed to leave things as they were for the time being, and the decision was relayed to Rachel through her mother. But in spite of the injunctions that she was not to chase after him, not to call him, and not to show up at his office, show up she did a few days later. She had to see him, she explained, and since her mother was out of town, she couldn't wait for her to get back. The matter was too important.

Steve was seated behind his desk when Rachel tumbled out her excuses, and he didn't rise. "What's this about, Rachel?"

"It's about Jamie, of course. What else?"

"Is anything the matter with him?"

"No, he's fine."

Steve looked annoyed. "Then what's so important that it couldn't wait for your mother to get back?"

"I want to thank you, Steve, for saying Jamie could go on thinking Ted's his father for now," she confided.

When she didn't continue, he looked even more annoyed. "And that's it? That's what was so important?"

She thrust her chin up in that defiant way she had. "Yes, that's it. Maybe you don't think it's so important because it doesn't mean that much to you having Jamie think Ted is his father."

"That's not true, Rachel, and you know it. Now please leave before I take back my okay." With a great show of humility, she left.

A few minutes later Steve left the office and drove home. He had intended to tell Alice about Rachel's visit as soon as he got there, but the more he thought about it, the more doubtful he became. Alice was extremely sensitive about Rachel, quick to insert things that weren't there between the lines. If he told her the truth, that Rachel had disobeyed his orders simply to thank him, she wouldn't believe it and he couldn't blame her. He wasn't so sure himself that Rachel wasn't up to her usual tricks, though what it was he didn't know. In the end he said nothing, and Rachel had once again accomplished what she wanted—to drive a wedge of deception and distrust into Steve and Alice's marriage.

As Christmas approached, Alice bought many presents for Steven, but the present she wanted above all to give him was not something you could order at Bryant's Department Store.

On Christmas Eve she put an armload of presents around the Christmas tree, a tall, full spruce set up in the bay window opposite the living-room fireplace. It had so many trinkets and lights on it you could barely see the tree. She had no sooner put the presents down than Steven started poking around among them.

"No fair peeking," Alice said.

"I'm looking for the one you said was on order."

"You won't find it there."

He looked up at her. "You mean you didn't get it?"

"Oh, no. I got it."

He poked around some more, holding up a box in red wrapping. "Is this it?"

She put her hands on her hips. "Didn't I just tell you you won't find it there?"

"People tell the most outrageous lies at Christmas time. Will it be here tomorrow?"

"No. It won't be here until next August. At least that's what the doctor said."

Steven dropped the package he was holding and straightened up, a look of wonder in his eyes. "Alice, are you going to have a baby?"

She smiled at him. "Yes, darling, I am. We are."

"Oh, Alice," he said, taking her in his arms. "That's the most wonderful present of all."

"Yes," she said, "I think so too."

She had never been happier.

Chapter Ten
Fall from Grace

During the Christmas holidays, a time of many cocktail and dinner parties, Mary Matthews began to realize that Pat's excessive drinking during Russ's and Cindy's engagement party had not been a one-time thing. On several occasions Mary noticed that Pat was having too much to drink. More ominous were the parties they never arrived at. She couldn't be certain it was Pat's drinking that kept them away, but she suspected it was.

After the holidays were over, Mary decided the time had come for her to do something. Whether or not John was fully aware of the problem, or had tried to do anything, she didn't know, but if he had tried, he had been unsuccessful. She called Pat to say she was coming over.

"Oh, Mother, this isn't really the best time for me. I have so much to do today."

Mary was prepared to be reasonable. "Then how about tomorrow, Pat?"

"Well, I don't know."

"Darling, I have to talk to you. It's important."

"What about?" Pat sounded suspicious.

"I'd rather not go into it on the phone."

"Not even to say what it's about?"

"No."

"I don't know," she said again, her voice trailing off.

"Let's make it tomorrow," Mary said firmly. "You can fit me in somewhere. I won't take that long."

"All right," Pat said, but she wasn't at all convincing.

The next morning Mary picked up the phone to tell her daughter she was on her way over, but then decided against it, sure Pat would have some excuse for putting her off. Instead, she put on her coat and went out. Pat came to the front door in answer to her ring. "Oh, Mother," she said, "I was just trying to call you to tell you I couldn't see you today after all."

"Well," Mary said, brushing past her into the foyer, "now that I'm here I hope you'll change your mind." She unbuttoned her coat, took it off, draped it over a chair, and went into the living room. Unless Pat chose to be rude, she would have no choice but to follow. Mary knew her daughter well.

"What do you want to see me about, Mother?" Pat entered reluctantly.

Mary patted the sofa cushion beside her. "Come sit with me, darling."

Pat sat down, but not beside her, choosing instead a chair opposite her mother.

"I want to talk to you about the twins," Mary said.

Pat looked perplexed and somewhat taken aback. "What about them?"

"First of all, I wanted you to remember how thrilled you were to have them, to have any child at all, when you were convinced you were sterile. Do you remember how thrilled you were?"

"Yes, well . . . Mother, of course I do. But I don't see what that has to do with . . . I mean, it wasn't any secret how thrilled I was. So why couldn't you say that over the phone?" Mary had at least captured her attention.

"I said I didn't want to go into it over the phone. I'm getting into it now."

"Then it isn't really the twins you want to talk about."

"Oh, yes, it is. Very much so. I'm concerned with their health and their welfare, along with your own. How much time do you spend with the twins, Pat?"

"As much as I can. It varies from day to day."

Mary nodded. "Yes, I'm sure it does. But yesterday, for instance."

"I told you yesterday was a very busy one for me."

"Meaning you saw very little of them?"

"Yes."

"And the day before?"

Pat was disturbed now. "Mother, what is this, some kind of inquisition?"

Mary sighed. "It's an attempt, a feeble one, I suppose, to try to get you to come to your senses and stop drinking your life away."

Pat's chin came up. "I'm not drinking my life away," she said stiffly.

"Darling, I've seen enough of you the last few weeks to know you're drinking far too much. Why didn't you show up at the Whitsons' Christmas party after saying you would?"

"I don't remember. Something came up."

"And the Sheldons' open house New Year's Day? Something you can't recall came up then too?"

Pat didn't answer.

"Darling, you never used to drink at all. What's happened to you?"

"Nothing's happened."

"Has John talked to you about your drinking?"

"No."

"But he must know about it. He could hardly live in the same house with you and not know about it."

The chin was up again. "All right, yes. He knows."

Mary studied her eldest daughter for a few moments. She wasn't as fragile-looking as Alice, but she didn't have Alice's emotional strength. "Darling, is it because of John that you're drinking the way you are?"

"No."

"Are you sure?"

"Yes, Mother, I'm sure, and I don't want to talk about it."

"All right," Mary said. "I suppose really it's none of my business. But the twins are, Pat. They're your children but they're my grandchildren, and I can't bear to see them neglected."

"They're not being neglected. Caroline takes excellent care of them."

"I'm sure she does," Mary agreed, "but she's not their mother. Do you want them to grow up thinking she is?"

"Mother, this is only a temporary thing."

"I don't call something that's been going on for over a year a temporary thing. Pat, go stand in front of a mirror and look at what you're doing to yourself. Then go upstairs to the nursery and stand in the doorway and look at what you're doing to those two darling babies of yours. Is this what you want for your children?"

Unexpectedly Pat buried her face in her hands, but

she didn't cry. Her face still hidden she said, "No, Mother, it's not what I want for them."

"Then, darling, please stop drinking. Please. For the twins' sake if not for your own. Pat, look at me."

Pat took her hands away from her face and tried to meet her eyes.

"Darling, think how you would have felt if I'd been a drunkard when you and Russ and Alice were growing up."

Pat looked as if she had been slapped. "Mother, I'm not a drunkard."

Mary kept a firm gaze on her daughter. "What do you call it then?"

Pat didn't answer but sat very still, her fingers clenched into fists. "All right. I'll stop drinking. You're right. I've let it get out of hand. I'll stop."

Mary broke into a smile and sighed as though everything were settled. "That's wonderful news, darling. Talk to the people at A.A. Get them to . . ."

Pat cut her off. "I don't need the help of A.A. I'm not an alcoholic, Mother. I've simply let myself get into the habit of drinking too much."

"And you can get out of the habit all by yourself, with no help from anybody?"

"That's right. I can." Pat stood up. "Let's stop discussing it, or all this talk *will* drive me to drink. Come upstairs and see the twins."

"That's the nicest invitation I've had all week!" she exclaimed.

Taking her daughter's arm, Mary tried to reassure her with her physical presence that all would be well. Together they went up to the nursery. Caroline greeted them both warmly. She was devoted to Michael and Marianne. *Sometimes*, Mary thought, *almost too devoted*. But she took excellent care of them.

The twins gurgled and slobbered and laughed when Mary tickled them. They never tired of peek-a-boo, but after almost an hour with them, Mary said she had to get back to the house. Jim had some accounting work in the neighborhood, and he was coming home for lunch.

As Pat helped her into her coat, Mary said, "Darling, if the struggle gets too much for you, give me, or somebody, a call. Will you, please?"

"Yes, Mother. I will. But don't worry about me. I'll be all right."

"I hope so, darling."

During the drive home, Mary reflected that at least the problem was out in the open now. She only wished Pat were not so proud. It was pride, she was sure, that kept her from admitting she was an alcoholic, that put her "above" the members of A.A. But maybe she could stop drinking all by herself. She had said she would stop, and when Pat said something, she meant it.

Mary's words had hit too close to home. Pat felt anxious, agitated, and began eyeing the liquor cabinet in the living room. When not having a drink began to get to her she did what she considered the most sensible thing she could do. She put on her hat and coat and went for a brisk walk. An hour later she was back home again, tired, cold, and still determined not to give in to the urge to drink.

She fixed lunch for herself but had no appetite. *Maybe*, she thought, *if I had one little drink—only one— that would perk up my appetite and see me through the rest of the day.* She fixed herself a watered-down Scotch and soda.

She enjoyed the drink, savored it. She had been right. It did perk up her appetite. She ate lunch and enjoyed that as well. Feeling better than she had in a long time Pat set about her afternoon chores, beginning with a thorough cleaning of the kitchen, shelves included.

She had been scouring and dusting for about an hour when she began wanting another drink. Thinking it must be nearing the end of the afternoon, she glanced at the clock, and was dismayed to see it was only two-thirty. Thinking the clock must be wrong, she went into the living room to check the grandfather clock. It too said two-thirty. She went back to her cleaning.

But the more she tried not to think about it, the more she wanted—no, *needed* a drink. She argued with herself, but to no avail. Finally, she gave up trying to clean the kitchen and sat in the living room, hoping to will away the urge to have a drink. Far from going away, it grew worse.

After sitting this way for some time, she burst into tears. As the late afternoon shadows lengthened, she sat there crying and feeling sorry for herself. Then she got up slowly, went to the liquor cabinet, and poured herself another Scotch and soda, stronger this time.

The last thing Rachel expected was that her own husband would help her in her campaign to get Steve Frame away from Alice. Not that Ted did it consciously, for he had no way of knowing what he was setting in motion. It all started early in the new year, on a Monday night—a slow night at the restaurant—when Ted and Rachel were having dinner with Ada. During the main course, Ted brought up a subject he'd mentioned when he and Rachel were first married—that he adopt Jamie as his son.

"Are you crazy?" Rachel blurted out. Knowing that

Ada liked Ted as much as she disliked Steve, Rachel turned on her. "Whose idea was this? Yours?"

"No, Rachel," Ted interrupted. "It was mine. But your mother and I have talked about it, and she thinks it's a good idea."

"I don't," Rachel retorted. "In the first place, Steve would never stand for it, and in the second . . ." Her voice trailed off.

"And in the second place, what?" Ada said, eyeing her daughter suspiciously.

Rachel tossed her head. "Never mind."

"I still think it's a good idea," Ted said.

"Good idea or not, Steve will never stand for it, and that's that," Rachel said. "Pass the potatoes, please."

Ted handed her the bowl. "It's not necessarily that's that. I might win the case," he said, "if we took it to court."

Dishing potatoes onto her plate, Rachel stopped, the spoon in midair. She stared at Ted, her brown eyes wide open. "Who said anything about going to court?"

"I did."

She thrust the spoon back into the mound of potatoes. "Who have you been talking to?"

"Nobody. Look, Rachel. I'm as good as being Jamie's father now. He thinks I'm his father. Whose idea was it to let him think so?" Ted seemed genuinely perplexed.

Rachel put her hands in her lap and said slowly, eyes fixed on her fork, "All right. It was mine. But I had to work like crazy to get Steve to agree to it, and he only said okay on a temporary basis. He'll never go along with your adopting Jamie. Never."

Ada knew only too well why Rachel had come up with this excuse. Any of Rachel's ideas were nothing more than ploys to keep her hold on Steve. By adopting Jamie, Ted could cut Rachel's only connection to Steve Frame, get Steve out of her daughter's life once and for all. And that was why Rachel was resisting it so mightily. *So much,* Ada thought, *for all Rachel's talk about having changed, about being in love with Ted, about being sorry for all the pain she'd brought to Alice. Talk was all it was.*

She noticed thankfully that Ted wasn't giving up. He took a new tack. "Rachel," he said, "who does Jamie live with?"

"He lives with us."

"And who do you consult with when something comes up about him?"

"Ordinarily, you. But if it were something big and important I'd go to Steve, the way I always have."

Ted arched his thick brown eyebrows. "Such as when?"

"Well," Rachel said, flustered, "I'm sure I can come up with some example." But she couldn't think of anything she wanted to admit to, and Ada sat mute as a stone. She fell back on bluster. "Well, never mind. It's all useless talk anyhow. Just forget about it."

Yet Rachel was unable to follow her own advice. Giving it some long, hard thought, she came to the conclusion that the idea had some great possibilities, beginning with still another opportunity to see Steve.

Or, better yet, she might be able to make him come to her.

She called him at home, hanging up the first two times, when Alice answered. On the third call, Steve picked up the phone.

"Steve, I have to talk to you."

He was so astonished he didn't answer her immediately. Alice, only a few feet away from him on the sofa, said, "Another wrong number, darling?"

Trying to think his way out of his dilemma, Steve said,

"No. It's one of my field men, calling from Chicago. I need to talk to him on the phone upstairs in the den, where my briefcase is." He spoke into the phone again. "Give me your number. I'll call you back in a few minutes." Hanging up the phone, he hurried upstairs. Once in his den, Steve breathed more easily. "Damn you, Rachel," he growled, "don't you pull a stunt like this again."

"It's no stunt," she said defensively. "I had to talk to you, unless you don't care if you lose Jamie."

Alice and Rachel both understood that Steve was deeply attached to his only child. One reason Alice had wanted this pregnancy so much was the hope that, by giving him a second child, and eventually another child or two, Steve's feelings for Jamie would be less intense.

"What do you mean?" he said, alarmed now. "What's happened to Jamie?"

"Nothing's happened to him," Rachel said. "He's fine. But you're not going to be so fine if you don't start doing something and doing it fast."

He was bewildered. "Rachel, what are you talking about?"

"I'm talking about you and Jamie. I'm not going to talk any more about it on the phone. Do you know where Jamie's nursery school is?"

"Of course I do."

"Then meet me in front of it tomorrow morning at ten o'clock."

Steve protested, but Rachel was adamant, and reiterated her vague warnings. At last he gave in and agreed to meet her. At ten o'clock the next day he stood outside the school as she drove up. It was a cold, raw February morning, so he got into her car, sitting as far away from her as possible. "What's this all about?" he said tensely.

"It's about Ted wanting to adopt Jamie as his son."

Steve stared at her in disbelief.

"He's prepared to go to court to do it, too. If it comes to that."

"Court? How far has this thing gone? Why wasn't I told anything before now?" Steve's temper was warming up.

"There wasn't anything to tell you, Steve. He brought it up the other night. He only said that about going to court when I told him you'd never stand for his adopting Jamie."

Steve nodded. "I wouldn't. What makes Ted think the court would be on his side?"

"Several things, starting with the fact that he lives with us. But the other night he made the point that I never consult with you when it comes to making decisions about Jamie. I talk to him about it, and he's right. I do talk to him about Jamie. Do you want to know why, Steve? Because you won't allow me to talk to you. So what do you have to say to that?"

As Rachel had anticipated, Steve remained broodingly quiet.

"So," she went on, "if you don't want to lose Jamie to Ted, then you've got to start meeting with me at least once in a while to talk about Jamie. Then, if Ted does go to court, I can say to the judge it's not true that I've never consulted you. I can even give him examples of the times I've done it."

"You have a point," Steve mused.

Rachel was careful to keep her voice neutral. "Well? Will you do it then, Steve?"

"I'll think about it, Rachel."

"I don't see what there is to think about." She shrugged impatiently.

"That's because you've already had time to do it. I've

just been hit with this."

"All right," she said. "Then think about it. But don't take all winter, or it will be too late."

"I won't," he promised. He got out of the car, then leaned in to say, "And don't call me, Rachel. I'll call you."

"Be sure you do," she said.

For an answer he closed the car door, walked to his own car, and drove away.

For a couple of weeks Steve didn't do more than think about the problem—in off moments, when he wasn't involved with office matters or people. At last, he took it up with John Randolph, asking John what he thought Ted's chances would be if the matter went to court.

John thought Ted's chances might be good and said so.

"Even if I contested him?" Steve said.

"Yes. Even if."

Steve walked to the window in his office that overlooked the streets below. "Then I've got a problem on my hands."

"Your real problem," John pointed out, "is Alice. No matter how little actual time you spend with Rachel discussing Jamie, Alice is going to see it as a threat."

Steve sighed. "I know that."

There was a light tap on his door, it opened, and Bernice came in, saying, "The specifications on this— oh, I'm sorry, Steve. I didn't realize you had somebody with you." She smiled at John. "How are you, John?"

"Fine, thanks, Bernice."

"I'll get back to you later, Steve." She smiled again and went out.

It seemed to Steve that more and more often lately Bernice found excuses to interrupt him when he was with John. John always seemed so stiff and uncomfortable around her that he wondered, not for the first time, if something was going on between them. Though John had always seemed completely devoted to Pat, he'd heard some rumors in the last few weeks that Pat had been hitting the bottle. Maybe John's involvement with Bernice—if he was involved with her—was the reason for Pat's drinking.

Steve sighed. Apparently he wasn't the only one with problems. To John he said, "I agree with what you said about Alice. That's the main reason I've been dragging my feet on this adoption business. Alice is very intelligent. Yet when it comes to Rachel, her intelligence gets blocked by her emotions."

John nodded. "Happens to the best of us."

"Try and see if you can come up with how to explain it to Alice, and I'll do the same. Then perhaps we'll put our heads together again and have something."

John agreed to that, and Steve postponed making a decision, hoping Ted would drop his adoption idea on his own. But Steve's doing nothing led to Rachel's doing something.

One day early in March Steve stayed home from the office to do some extra research in his upstairs den on a construction project. Construction work was still the core of Steven Frame Enterprises, and Steven Frame the man was still at heart a construction engineer.

Often when he worked at home Alice found little household chores for him to do. Today she asked his help in cleaning out and rearranging the big walk-in closet in the downstairs hall. She never had to ask twice. He loved being with her and helping her.

While they were doing it he went to the kitchen for a glass of water, and the phone rang. It was Rachel. She said she had to see him immediately or he could forget about winning Ted's court fight for Jamie. When Steve protested that he couldn't go anywhere right now, that he was busy, she said, "Okay. Then hang up so I can call again. And if you answer, I'll keep calling until Alice answers, and I'll tell her everything."

When he went back to the closet Alice said, "Who was it, darling?"

"Uh . . . that same field man from Chicago I've talked to several times now. I forgot. He's been here the last few days, and I told him I'd meet him at his motel this morning and drive him to the airport so we could have a final conference before he returns to Chicago."

"Then you'd better get going, or you won't have time to say more than good-bye."

Steve started to fold the aluminum ladder he'd been using to hand boxes down to Alice. "No," she said, "leave it, darling or we'll never get back to this job."

"I'll leave it as long as you don't get any bright ideas about finishing this job by yourself."

"No. I won't do that. I'll wait for you. I promise."

"All right, then." He kissed her good-bye and left to meet Rachel in front of Jamie's nursery school again, ready to clobber her if this was one of her tricks.

It wasn't a trick. She had investigated various private schools in Bay City and had been told by everybody that the best one was Holyoke. "But if we want to apply to Holyoke, the deadline is today."

"Rachel," Steve protested, "Jamie's only in nursery school."

"I know that. But the best way to get into Holyoke, the only sure way, is to start him in the nursery school there. There's already a waiting list for kindergarten."

"Oh. Well, all right then."

"Also, as long as you're here, Steve, what about the

other decision I've been waiting for? Are you going to agree to meet with me once in a while to talk about Jamie?"

"All right. Yes." He made up his mind then and there.

Rachel smiled. "That's wonderful. But what will you tell Alice?"

"I'll tell her the truth. And the sooner the better."

Back in his own car Steve drove aimlessly, trying to decide how to break the news to Alice, but he couldn't think of any best way other than simply to tell her. He called the house to suggest taking her out to lunch, but there was no answer. Then he remembered she already had a lunch date with her mother and sister. The rumors about Pat's drinking were true, and this luncheon was part of Mary's scheme to help Pat lick the problem by keeping her occupied and in somebody's company.

At almost the same time Mary Matthews called Alice to confirm the time and got no answer either. Worried, she and Pat drove out to the house and found Alice unconscious on the hall floor. Disregarding her promise to Steve, she had tried to finish the closet by herself. She was putting a heavy box on the top shelf when she fell off the ladder. The box fell on top of her, rupturing her spleen.

Mary summoned an ambulance and Alice was rushed to the hospital, where her spleen was removed. Sadly, she lost the baby as well.

Steve knew nothing about any of this until he turned up at John's law offices that afternoon for a scheduled meeting with him at two o'clock. Then he rushed to the hospital.

Alice was coming out of the anesthesia, and groggy as she was, she was determined to go home.

"Darling," Steve said, holding her hand, "you can't go home. Not yet. You've had an operation. They took out your spleen."

She gave him a groggy smile. "As long as they didn't take the baby."

"Alice. Darling."

She frowned. "Steven, they didn't take our baby, did they?"

"They tried awfully hard not to, darling. They wanted in the worst way to save it, but . . ." He swallowed and couldn't go on.

Alice's eyes were like deep pools filled with tears. "Oh, Steven, Steven. It was all my fault."

He shook his head. "No. Not your fault. Mine. I shouldn't have gone out and left you."

"I shouldn't have tried to finish the closet by myself. Oh, Steven."

"Hush, darling. I still have you. That's what counts the most."

A nurse came in to tell him he would have to go now. He could come back later. He nodded and bent to kiss Alice. "I'll be back, darling. You rest."

Chapter Eleven
Beginning of the End

While Alice was recuperating in the hospital, Gerald Davis sold the Riverboat over in Somerset and moved to Bay City to help Ted run the Fireside Inn. Since Rachel had always wanted to be near her father, having him around on a day-to-day basis helped make up for all the earlier disappointments. Secretly, she was also pleased when he confided that he thought Ted Clark was a loser and that every time she met with Steve to talk about Jamie she should try to make some time with him for herself.

She wouldn't admit even to her father that she was already doing her best to break down Steve's resistance, a resistance she felt—and always had—was only an act on his part, conscious or unconscious.

Alice went home from the hospital depressed over losing the baby. Her obstetrician had said that she had to wait at least a year before trying to get pregnant again. When the depression dragged on, she went back to see the doctor and burst into tears in his office.

When she apologized for doing so, the doctor said,

"It's better to give in to your grief. It will help you get over it."

Alice shook her head and wiped her eyes. "Nothing helps."

"Maybe you should go back to work," he said. "Then you won't have time to brood."

His suggestion appealed to her. Anything was better than moping around the house all day thinking about the baby she'd lost, fearful it was the only baby she would ever have. So she went back to nursing.

One afternoon Jamie was brought into the emergency room. He had been bitten by a copperhead while on an outing with Steve. The emergency-room treatment saved Jamie's life, but Alice, who was on staff at the time, found out that Rachel was also there when it happened. Her trust in Steve was badly damaged, and her marriage nearly destroyed altogether.

When Steve was able to explain to her why he had been with Rachel—to protect his rights as Jamie's father—and why he couldn't explain it to her sooner—because of her upset over losing the baby—they were reconciled. Still, their relationship wasn't what it had once been. And if Alice had been overly sensitive to Rachel before, she was now almost unapproachable where Rachel was concerned.

John Randolph drew up an agreement for all the interested parties to sign. Steve would see Jamie once a week, as before, but he would have no contact with Rachel—also, as before. The only new element was that Ted would give up his attempts to adopt Jamie.

Rachel wasn't happy with the agreement, and signed it only because she had no choice. But one afternoon in early September, when Ada arrived at Rachel's apartment to take Jamie to Steve's office, Rachel said it wasn't convenient.

"But you signed an agreement, Rachel. You have to live up to it."

"I didn't sign any agreement saying Steve could take Jamie anywhere he pleased."

Ada looked up. "What are you talking about? Where did Steve take Jamie?"

"He took him to his house."

"How do you know that?"

"Jamie told me. He met Alice and he likes her."

"What's wrong with that?"

"I don't want Jamie anywhere near Alice, anymore than Alice wants me anywhere near Steve. You can bet that it's Alice's doing that I'm not allowed to see Steve. It certainly isn't his. We were doing perfectly well together until Miss Dresden China Doll found out about it."

And protest as Ada did, Rachel stood her ground. Steve wasn't going to see Jamie again unless Rachel knew in advance where he was taking him and who he was going to be seeing, and she told her mother to tell Steve that.

As Ada had expected, Steve was not pleased when she turned up at his office without Jamie. "Rachel signed an agreement," he said.

Ada sighed. "Yes, I know that, Steve. I reminded her of that myself."

"Well?"

She sighed again. "If I'd ever been able to make Rachel listen to reason, none of what's happened would ever have happened in the first place, starting with Rachel chasing after you when she was still married to Russ."

Steve picked up the phone. "She had better listen to me."

"But you're not supposed to talk to her at all."

"And she's not supposed to keep me from seeing my son." But he replaced the phone in its cradle, thinking he would speak to John Randolph about this, get him to intercede. After all, that was what he paid John for—to handle his legal affairs.

After Ada left his office Steve tried to concentrate on the set of plans laid out on the drawing table, but the more he thought about Rachel and her tricks the angrier he got. He picked up the phone and called her apartment. When there was no answer, he called the Fireside Inn. Gerald Davis answered.

"This is Steve Frame. Is Rachel there?"

"No, Steve, she isn't. Can I take a message?"

"Yes. Would you ask her to call me, please, here at the office?"

"Consider it done."

When Gerald hung up, Rachel, sitting beside him at the bar, said, "Who's the 'she' who isn't here?"

Her father smiled. "You, honey. You."

She frowned. "That was Steve calling me?" She reached for the phone. "Why did you do that?"

Her father took the receiver out of her hand. "Trust me, Rachel. I know what I'm doing."

"Maybe you'll explain it to me, then, so I'll know too," she commanded.

Her father winked. "It's called strategy. You know Steve has to be angry at you for not letting Jamie visit him."

"Yes? So?"

"So let him get a little angrier when you don't even return his phone calls. Then when you're ready to see him, you'll be in a position to get what you want."

Rachel was still eyeing the phone. "How can you be so sure?"

"You wait. You'll see."

A couple of days later, after Steve had left several more messages and Gerald had restrained Rachel from calling him, he gave her the go-ahead. She reached him at his office, and said she would come there at the end of the day to discuss his visitation rights with him. Exasperated and reluctant, Steve finally agreed.

"Well," she said to her father as she was leaving to keep her appointment, "wish me luck."

He did more than that. He called the nurses' station on Alice's floor of the hospital. To the nurse who answered he said, "I want to leave a message for Mrs. Frame. I'm calling for her husband. He would like her to pick him up at his office on her way home tonight."

"Right," the nurse said. "I'll tell her."

When Rachel arrived at Steve's office he was upstairs in his old bachelor apartment working on some drawings and had turned on the radio. Not wanting to be alone with her there he suggested they go down one floor to his office.

"What's the matter?" she taunted. "Are you afraid of me?" She had draped herself on his sofa, and was wearing the same kind of skin-tight outfit she'd had on the night she seduced him. "It's like old times being here with you, Steve," Rachel said.

He was having no more of that and kept his distance. "We're not here to talk about old times, Rachel. We're here to talk about Jamie and why you're refusing to let me see him."

"I'm not refusing to let you see him. There's nothing I want more than for you and Jamie to be close. I'd like us to be close too, Steve, you and me, like we once were."

"Rachel, the only thing that brought us together was my own misery and loneliness, and I'd give anything to have that night back to live over again. I can tell you it wouldn't be spent the same way it was. Far from it."

"I don't believe that, Steve, and deep down I don't think you believe it either."

At that moment, unknown to either of them, Alice came up from Steve's office and entered the shadowy foyer of the apartment. Having received the message at the hospital, she went to his office to wait, and heard sounds from his bachelor apartment. Knowing he sometimes worked there when he wanted to be undisturbed, she took the elevator up. Now she stood frozen, listening to Steve and Rachel talking in the dimly lit apartment, their voices mingling with the music that filled the room.

"I've always felt close to you, Steve," Rachel was saying. "All those times when Alice thought you were in Somerset on business, when in fact you were with me and Jamie, we had some wonderful times together."

"Rachel," he protested, "this isn't talking about Jamie. It serves no purpose that I can see."

"Steve," Rachel said, "I can understand how you feel you have to pretend you don't care for me when there are other people around. But now it's just you and me."

"Rachel."

"No. Let me say it. That day when Alice lost her baby, and you were with me, I've never felt closer to any other man in my life than I did then to you."

Before Steve had a chance to respond to that, Alice turned and fled. As far as she was concerned, she had heard all she needed to. She drove home numb with shock. It was Rachel Steven had been with when she lost their baby! Not the field man. More than likely the field man had never existed.

When she got home she hesitated only briefly. If she

waited for Steven to explain what Rachel and he had been doing together this afternoon—assuming he would even try to explain—then she would be doing what she'd done before: she would let him talk her out of leaving him because he loved her and she loved him, which was certainly true enough.

She ran upstairs to their bedroom, packed some clothes and other personal effects into a suitcase, and called a taxi to get her.

When Steven reached home she was gone.

With Russ's prompting, Cindy began taking better care of herself. She even managed to put back a few pounds she had lost, giving Russ the impression that she was regaining her health.

"You're the only doctor I need, Russ," she had said. "All I want is you and my old job back."

"The only reason I'll let you have it," he told her, "is so I can keep an eye on you."

After reconciling with her beloved Russ and returning to her job as receptionist at his and Dan Shearer's clinic, Cindy was as happy as she had ever been in her young life. In fact her health was deteriorating. Cindy was aware of it but, frightened that her physical condition might be even worse than she imagined, she did nothing about it. She was careful to say nothing to Russ or her mother or brother that indicated in any way all was not as well as it seemed with her.

Russ was a very able internist and should have seen for himself that her health was becoming more and more precarious. But he was so involved with his clinic patients, and so full of plans for Cindy and himself and their upcoming marriage, he couldn't see what was right in front of him.

They were planning an October wedding, with a

Caribbean honeymoon in Steve Frame's house in St. Croix. Even after Alice's disappearance—she had left Bay City without telling even her parents where she was—Steve was quick to reassure the young couple, saying that they shouldn't postpone the wedding and that the house was still there for them; he'd be upset if they didn't use it.

"It's sweet of him to think of us when he must be out of his mind with worry over Alice," Cindy said.

"Yes, it is," Russ agreed.

"Did he mention her?"

Russ shook his head. "No, and I didn't have the heart to ask."

Cindy shivered. "Why do you think Alice left him?"

Russ ran his fingers through his glossy hair and sighed. "I don't know. But I suspect she was running from something."

Cindy frowned up at him. "Why do you say that?"

"Because that's Alice. Always has been. When she's upset, instead of confronting what causes it, she runs away from it."

"I hope he hears from her soon. I hate to think of them being so unhappy."

"Yes. So do I. Well, I've got a patient waiting. You going to have lunch with me today?" He chucked her under her chin.

"When you ask me like that," Cindy said, grinning, "how can I refuse?"

Cindy's best meals were those she ate with Russ, something he would have been less proud of had he known she skipped breakfast so she'd be better able to eat a good lunch with him.

Occasionally, to please Cindy, Russ took her to the Fireside Inn for dinner so she could see her brother. Russ didn't like going because Rachel was often there for dinner as well—to Rachel, the best thing about her husband's owning a restaurant was that she could eat dinner out without having to pay for it. Though Russ harbored no desire for Rachel whatsoever, seeing her was still a painful reminder of all she had put him through. She made it worse by always coming over to sit with them, prattling endlessly about Jamie this and Jamie that, totally insensitive to Russ's feelings.

Cindy could sense Russ's discomfort, and would try to distract Rachel. For her brother's sake too, she tried to like her sister-in-law, but it wasn't particularly easy.

Rachel insisted on giving a little dinner party for Russ and Cindy at the restaurant one night about two weeks before they were to be married. Because of Ted, they agreed to it. It was for a Saturday night, and since the clinic closed early on Saturdays, Cindy went home to get dressed for the party.

While she was showering she began feeling breathless. She grabbed hold of the shower rail and held on tight, trying to get her breath back, telling herself to relax, to do the breathing exercises Russ had taught her when she had first gone to the clinic to see him as a patient. In a few minutes she was breathing normally enough to finish her shower and climb out over the tub railing and, once outside, to stand on the mat beside the tub, toweling herself dry.

She was standing next to her bed, pulling on her stockings, when she began feeling breathless again, only this time she had some chest pains as well. Frightened, she sat down on the edge of the bed. In a few minutes the pain stopped, and her breathing became more regular.

She told herself that she was having anxiety attacks because of Rachel's dinner party tonight. When Russ came to pick her up at seven, he took her hands in his and said, "Sweetheart, do you feel okay?"

"Oh, I guess I'm just a bit anxious," she replied.

"I don't blame you," he said. "So am I. I wish Rachel had never come up with this idea or that we hadn't given in to it."

"Me too," Cindy said. "But it's too late now."

Rachel's idea of a little dinner party was thirty people chosen on the basis of their social status, people she wanted to impress—and to be socially indebted to her. Some of them Russ and Cindy didn't even know.

She had invited Steve, hoping he might come alone, but he had no intention of walking into another one of Rachel's setups—at least not voluntarily. As a concession to Russ, Rachel invited Pat and John Randolph, and they came, sitting at the same table as Russ and Cindy. But they seemed to Cindy to be as unhappy to be there as she and Russ were. More, they seemed to be under a strain, bright and smiling when anybody was looking, tense and drawn in their more private moments.

Cindy got through the evening with no further episodes or breathlessness or chest pains. However, when the dinner party was finally over and she was home again, alone in her bedroom getting undressed for bed, she had another attack. This one was more frightening than the others, partially because she had no sensible-sounding excuse for it.

She considered getting dressed again and going to Bay City Memorial's emergency room, but then the chest pains passed, and her breathing became normal, so she finished undressing and climbed into bed.

The next day, after Cindy and Russ attended church with his parents, the four of them went to look at an apartment for the young couple.

"I think it's terrific," Jim Matthews said as they

trooped through the empty rooms, their heels tapping on the bare floors, their voices echoing off the bare walls.

"Yes," Mary said, "it's really very nice."

"What do you say, Cindy?" Russ asked. "Shall we take it?"

"You make the decision, Russ. But if it will help you any, I like the apartment very much."

Russ hugged her to him. "That's good enough for me. We'll take it."

They decided to celebrate by having lunch together—and not at the Fireside Inn. They went to a restaurant on the wharf that specialized in Sunday brunches. "We won't tell them we've had breakfast," Jim said, and the others laughed.

"So, Russ and Cindy," Jim continued, "here's to your new apartment! And we can also celebrate the letter we received from Alice yesterday."

"Oh, yes!" Mary chimed in. "She still doesn't want to tell us where she is, but at least I know she's all right."

They each had a Bloody Mary to start, and when Cindy began feeling a bit woozy midway through her scrambled eggs, she blamed it on the vodka. When the wooziness returned that night, again as she was getting undressed for bed, she told herself she had better see a cardiologist. The next afternoon she did.

He was a man in his sixties, a kindly, fatherly man, who broke the bad news to her as gently as he could. He put an arm around her and held her to him while she buried her face against his chest and cried.

She went from his office to the clinic, sitting at the reception desk until the last patient of the day had gone. Then she walked quietly into Russ's office. His face lit up at the sight of her. Seeing this was almost as terrible for her as the cardiologist's prognosis.

"Sit down, sweetheart," Russ said, scribbling on a chart. "I'll be through here in a sec." He closed the chart and filed it away. "Now. What are our plans for this evening?"

"Russ, have you paid the deposit on the apartment?"

He hesitated. "I've made out the check, but I haven't mailed it. Why?"

"Russ, I can't marry you."

He got up from his desk and came around it to her. "What do you mean, you can't marry me? What has Ted done now?"

"He hasn't done anything."

"Then who has?"

Cindy shook her head. "Nobody."

Taking her by the arms, he pulled her gently to her feet. "Then why can't you marry me? You still love me, don't you? That hasn't changed, has it?"

She wanted to lie to him but she couldn't. "No, that hasn't changed."

"Then why can't you marry me?"

"Because I'm not the right person for you, Russ."

He tightened his hold on her. "Cindy, stop talking nonsense. We've been through all this before."

"I know, but it's not the same now."

"What's not the same? Cindy, what's happened?"

She couldn't bear to have him pity her, but she couldn't think what to say to him.

Then suddenly, without warning, the breathlessness and the chest pains came back. This time they were unbearable. "Oh, my God," Russ said. "Are you having an attack?"

Unable to speak, she nodded.

"Here," he said. "Sit down. Try to relax. You're going to be all right. I'll get help." He grabbed a blanket and wrapped it around her. "It's important you keep warm."

He dialed the hospital's emergency room and told them to send an ambulance. Then he went to the drug cabinet and came back with two tablets and a glass of water. "Here. Take these."

Even before the ambulance got there she was feeling a bit better. Russ rode with her to the hospital, staying at her side while a cardiologist there stabilized her.

He learned, from seeing her X rays and reading the notations in her chart, what she had learned that day from the kindly cardiologist—that she had a badly diseased heart, and—in those pretransplant days—only a short time to live.

He sat by her bed, holding her hand in one of his, using the other to stroke her face, not saying much.

When the time came for him to leave, he said, "I love you, Cindy, and I'm going to marry you." He squeezed her hand. "Take care, my darling. I'll be back first thing in the morning."

Leaving the hospital, where Cindy was now in the Coronary Care Unit, he wandered aimlessly about for a time, trying to absorb the shock of the cardiologist's prognosis, fighting against believing it, knowing he had to.

He drove home. His parents were out and, not wanting to be alone, he went to see Pat and John. There was so little light coming from the windows that he thought they must be out too. Yet John came to the door when he rang the bell.

He looked as distraught as Russ felt, but motioned him in. "I'm sorry, Russ. I'm afraid things are not in very good shape here." Russ walked ahead of him into the living room.

Pat was sitting on the sofa, drunk. She waved him

in. "Join the fight. We give as good as we take here. Isn't that so, my darling husband?"

"Pat," John said, "I don't think Russ wants to know about all of this."

"You mean," she said, "you hope he doesn't want to know all about you. Because he can't see what you've been up to—only what I have."

Before John could answer, Russ put a hand up. "I'm sorry for bursting in like this. I should have called first to see if this was a convenient time for me to come by."

"Why should you apologize?" Pat asked. "Nobody else around here does. I mean, John was just telling me he . . ."

"Be quiet, please, Pat," Russ said brusquely. "I'll say what I have to say and then get out of here. Cindy had a heart attack a few hours ago. She's in the CCU at the hospital."

"Oh, Russ," Pat said, sobering. "How awful—"

John moved next to Russ and put his hand on his arm. "What can we do?"

"You can let me finish. She has a very badly diseased heart and only a short time to live. But I intend to marry her all the same and if you can straighten yourselves out long enough to be our witnesses, I'd appreciate it."

Without waiting for a response from either of them, he left the room and the house.

Pat and John stared after him, then at each other wordlessly.

Chapter Twelve

Last Rites

A few days after Cindy's admission to the hospital, she was moved from the CCU to a private room. The cardiologist at first opposed the move, saying she needed to be in the Coronary Care Unit, her situation was too desperate.

"Are you saying," Cindy asked him gently, "that if I stay here in the unit that eventually I'll get well enough to leave it?"

He looked down at her. He knew she was aware of her condition. "No, I'm not saying that."

"Then let me have a room of my own, at least until after Russ and I are married."

"All right," he said. "At least until then."

Just as the cardiologist had opposed the move, Cindy had at first opposed the marriage, even as she held hands with Russ and let him caress and kiss her. "I don't see why you want to marry me," she said.

"For the same reason I've wanted to marry you all along," he answered her. "Because I love you."

There were tears in her dark eyes. "But is love enough, Russ?"

His own eyes glistened. "For us it will have to be, darling."

A very sober, shaken Pat had called Russ the morning after his visit to say that if he and Cindy still wanted them, she and John would be honored to be their witnesses.

"Yes, of course we still want you, Pat," Russ said, "but don't feel that you have to do it. I'm sorry I spoke so sharply last night. I was in a pretty terrible state."

"Russ, please don't apologize, and please don't think about it anymore. Just let us know when you want us to be there. Okay?"

"Yes. And thanks, Sis."

"I'm the one who's going to end up thanking you," she said.

The wedding took place on a mid-October afternoon, a little ahead of the date they had originally settled on, the cardiologist having told Russ not to wait too long. Cindy had a corsage of red roses pinned to the little white lace jacket she wore over her hospital gown. Pat had a corsage of yellow roses pinned to the jacket of her soft brown wool suit.

The minister was the Reverend Mr. Hilton, the pastor of the church all the Matthews family attended. It was a simple and moving ceremony, especially when Reverend Hilton got to the exchange of vows, when first Russ and then Cindy promised "to have and to hold, from this day forward, for better, for worse, for richer, for poorer, in sickness and in health, to love and to cherish, and, forsaking all others, cling to each other until death do us part."

At the conclusion of the ceremony Russ kissed Cindy, and then Pat and John kissed her. After Pat and John had left the room, Cindy's mother and brother, who had stayed outside in the hall to listen to the ceremony, came in separately to kiss the bride, not realizing they were kissing her good-bye.

When everybody except Russ had gone, the cardiologist came in to offer his congratulations and to check on his patient. Cindy was concerned that he would have her taken back to the CCU now, and she begged for a little more time alone with Russ.

"All right, Cindy," the cardiologist said sympathetically. "We won't move you just yet." He nodded to Russ to step outside with him. "I think if I were you I'd stay here with her. It doesn't look good at all."

"I was planning to anyhow," Russ said.

He went back into the room and sat down beside the bed, holding Cindy's hand in his.

"Thank you for doing this for me, Russ," she said.

"I did it as much for myself as for you, Cindy. And there's something else I'm going to do for you and for me."

"What?" she asked.

"I'm going to train in cardiology. I'm only sorry I didn't do it before now."

She smiled. "Don't think of it that way, darling. You couldn't have helped me even if you had."

"No, I don't suppose I could have."

She tightened her hold on his hand. "But I think it's wonderful that you're going to do it now. Russ, darling—" Cindy smiled at him.

"Yes?"

"Please don't leave me tonight."

"No, I won't. Is the pain bad?"

"A little."

"Do you want me to call the cardiologist?"

"No. I want you to stay with me."

"Don't think anymore about it. I'm not going anywhere."

At dinnertime, when an aide brought in her tray, Cindy only shook her head. Russ took the tray and put it out in the hall.

About an hour later, she said, "Russ, I love you."

He squeezed her hand. "And I love you, Cindy."

Shortly after that her hand went limp. Russ stood up and put his stethoscope to her heart. It had stopped.

When Pat got home from the wedding ceremony, she went straight to the liquor cabinet. That didn't surprise John. What did surprise him was what she did next. She took two bottles of Scotch from the cabinet, walked into the kitchen, and poured their contents down the sink. Then she returned to the liquor cabinet, collected a bottle of gin, one of vodka, one of bourbon, and one of rye, and did the same with them. Next to go were the liqueurs and after that the wine. The Randolph house was now bereft of alcohol, except for the rubbing kind upstairs in the medicine chest.

"You can do what you want to," she said to John, standing in silence watching her, "but I'm through with feeling so sorry for myself that I want to drink myself out of existence. The people who have a right to feel sorry for themselves are Russ and Cindy and Alice and Steve, and none of them are alcoholics."

He moved toward her. "Darling, I think what you're doing is . . ."

She cut him off. "Stay where you are, John. What I said was not meant to be an invitation."

"But darling, I only . . ."

"You can stop that too. You can only have one darling. I didn't marry you to lend you out. So you make your decision about that, and then we'll see what we have to say to each other."

"I've already decided," he said. He moved toward

her again, and would have taken her in his arms, but she slipped away from him.

"I decided almost a year ago to quit drinking, but I didn't, did I? There's a little more to this than talk, John."

She was already moving past him out of the kitchen. "Where are you going?" he asked.

"To get the telephone directory to call Alcoholics Anonymous. Mother was right when she said I needed help. I do need it. I can't lick this thing by myself."

Listed in the directory was the twenty-four-hour hotline A.A. maintained. Pat called the number and was told somebody would be out to see her as soon as he or she could get there.

A woman came in about twenty minutes. She was around Pat's age, and was as socially prominent in Bay City as Pat herself. Pat stared at her in astonishment. The woman nodded. "I know. With people like us it's just a 'drinking problem.' The alcoholics are the ones in the bars or the gutters. At least that's what we tell ourselves, when we're not insisting to various members of the family that this is only a temporary thing."

Impulsively Pat hugged her. "You make me feel I'm going to beat it."

The woman smiled at her. "You *are* going to. I did it and you can too. Now. Let's sit down and get acquainted."

John didn't have a hotline to turn to. Help in extricating oneself from an extramarital entanglement isn't as easy to come by. He could, of course, have gone to Reverend Hilton or to a marriage counselor, but he was too ashamed to tell anybody he knew, and he couldn't see the point of consulting somebody he didn't know.

The morning after the wedding ceremony he went to the office as usual. Because of his absence yesterday afternoon there were some messages on his desk that had to be attended to. That done, he called Bernice. "I have to talk to you," he said.

"You make it sound terribly important," she said lazily, invitingly.

For the first time since he'd known her, her seductiveness irritated him. *She turns it off and on like a faucet*, he thought. "If it's convenient," he said, "I can stop by your office later this morning. How about eleven?"

"Eleven would be fine."

On another occasion when he had stopped by her office at eleven, they had told Steve they were having an early lunch together. Instead, they had gone to her apartment for a different kind of sustenance. When he arrived at her office today, she seemed to expect the same scenario.

John sat down across her desk from her. "Bernice," he said, "I'm going back to my wife. If she'll have me."

Bernice smiled. "And if she won't?"

"Then I'll do whatever I can to make her change her mind. I'm sorry."

She said softly, "I didn't expect it to last forever."

"Maybe," he said, "you don't want that kind of alliance."

"Maybe not," she agreed. "Well," she said, standing up, "there's no point in dragging it out, is there?"

He too stood up. "No. None at all."

She smiled again, this time more broadly. "And it isn't as though I'll never set eyes on you again." She glanced at her desk calendar. "In fact, we have a meeting with Steve this afternoon."

"Right. See you then."

Leaving her office he thought to himself that Bernice only half-believed they were through. There was only one way to prove to her he meant what he said, and that was to stay away from her.

Before long, John and Pat were reconciled. As soon as Pat was satisfied that John was no longer seeing Bernice and felt that she was at least partly responsible for his becoming involved with her to begin with, she returned to the master bedroom. There she also returned to her role as his wife and sexual partner, hushing his apologies, kissing away his protestations of guilt, her own desire for alcohol lessening as her desire for John was roused and then satisfied.

"Darling," he said to her one night as they lay in each other's arms, their passion spent, "let's not ever get separated like that again, all right?"

"Never, darling," Pat agreed. "Never again."

And both of them believed they never would.

Steve was still trying to pick up the pieces of his life and put them back together. When Alice wrote her parents saying she was all right, she also revealed in the same letter that she had left Steven because she found out he'd been betraying her.

Jim Matthews, who was more sympathetic to Steve than Mary was, drove out to his house to show him the letter. Steve read it, silently. "I don't understand what she means," he said after he had read through it a second time. "I wasn't betraying her. Not in any way, shape, or form."

His father-in-law said, "But Steve, she couldn't make something like that up."

"No. She couldn't and wouldn't. There has to be some misunderstanding somewhere. If only I knew where Alice was so I could go to her and talk to her. If I could just find out what the problem is. I can't very well resolve the misunderstanding until I know what it is."

But Alice's whereabouts remained a mystery to all concerned. One person, however, was delighted by the way events were unfolding.

The problem, as far as Rachel was concerned, was the same as it had always been—Steve's resistance to her—except for that once. Whenever Rachel tried to cozy up to Steve, she came up against a stone wall. He wanted nothing to do with her and said so.

Her father tried to make light of it. Sitting with Rachel one afternoon in a booth at the Fireside Inn, he said to her, "Things have changed for Steve now that Alice has left him. It's up to you to take advantage of that."

Rachel was gloomy. "Steve keeps saying Alice will come back."

"Do you see any sign of it?"

"No."

"Well, there you are."

Rachel sighed. "That's what I keep telling myself, but where I am is nowhere."

He shook his head. "Rachel, this is no time for you to give up—not when everything's set up for you."

Rachel frowned at him. "What do you mean, set up?"

Her father tried to cover his near admission of the helping hand he'd given her. "I mean now Alice is gone. She's always been your stumbling block, hasn't she?"

"Yes."

"She's removed herself. It's your signal to move in."

Rachel sighed again. "I wish it were so simple."

Not too long after Rachel had that conversation with her father, Alice did two things to simplify things for Rachel. First, she called her parents on Christmas. She said she was well, settled, and working for a family, tutoring their son who was unable to attend a regular school because of a heart condition. She didn't mention Steve, nor did she call him.

Steve had always regarded Alice as being fair, but as more and more time went by and there was no word from her, he began to feel she was being very unjust.

One afternoon in Steve's office, John Randolph tried to be sympathetic. "I know what it is to have to wait like this," he offered.

Steve's bitter response was, "Wait for what, John? To be forgiven for what I didn't do?"

The second thing Alice did was send her father out once again to Steve's house. He arrived a little after seven o'clock one night. Steve greeted him at the door. "Come in, Jim. What's up?"

"It's more bad news, I'm afraid, Steve."

Alarm flooded through him. "Is it Alice?

Jim put a hand on his arm. "No, no. Alice is all right. I'm sorry. I didn't mean to frighten you. It's bad news of another kind."

"What kind then?"

"Alice wrote asking for her personal belongings."

"I see. All right. I'll send them to her. But I have to know where she is—"

"She doesn't want you to send them, Steve. She wants me to pack them up for her and store them at our house."

"In other words," Steve said, "she still doesn't want me to know where she is."

"I guess not," Jim said. "I'm sorry, Steve."

Steve headed for the stairs. "Come on upstairs, then. I'll help you pack."

In the master bedroom Steve took a couple of suitcases out of a closet and opened them on the bed. The two men began packing Alice's belongings into them.

"I guess," Steve said at one point, "this means she isn't coming back to me."

"I wish I could say otherwise," Jim said.

Steve shook his head. "I'll never understand it—how she could go off like that, without a word of explanation? And then to stay away all this time—and still with no word."

"I think," Jim said, "she doesn't trust herself to get in touch with you. She cares too much about you."

Steve stared at his father-in-law in open disbelief. "What kind of sense does that make?"

Jim shrugged. "I guess to you, not any."

"That's right," Steve asserted. "Not any."

When they had finished packing, they took the suitcases down to Jim's car. "Oh, and there's one other thing," Jim said. "Mary would like to have her rocking chair back. You know, the one she gave Alice."

At first Steve couldn't think what rocking chair Jim was talking about, but then he remembered. "All right. I'll go and get it."

The rocking chair was up in the room he and Alice had outfitted as a nursery. He hadn't been in the room since Alice had left. It was almost more than he could bear to go in there now, but he gritted his teeth and did it, not turning a light on, feeling his way among the shadowy outlines of the crib, the changing table, the little dresser. He picked up the rocking chair and went out, closing the door behind him.

After Jim left the house, Steve poured himself a drink.

A new development was unfolding, something to make Rachel's campaign for Steve easier. For some time Ted had been talking of moving to Chicago, expecting as a matter of course to take Rachel and Jamie with him. At last he had found the restaurant he wanted and had gone there to start it—and start looking for somewhere the three of them could live. Rachel let Ted assume she would join him in Chicago, but she had no intention of going. Her father applauded that decision.

It was her father, in fact, who initiated the final move in pushing Steve into Rachel's arms again. He called her apartment the night after Jim Matthews took Alice's belongings home with him to say that Steve was in the Fireside Inn sitting alone in a booth, drinking. Why didn't Rachel come along and see what she could do?

Rachel took only ten minutes to dress in one of her most enticing outfits and take Jamie over to her mother's house to spend the night.

When she arrived at the Inn, Steve was still there, still drinking. "Hello, Rachel," he said when she appeared at the booth. He sounded neither friendly nor unfriendly.

"Do you mind if I join you, Steve?"

He waved a hand. "It's a free country. Besides, it's your restaurant." When she slid into the seat across from him he said, "I suppose you've heard that Alice is never coming back to me."

"I know that's what you think."

"It's more than what I think. It's true."

Rachel gambled a little. "I never did think Alice was right for you."

"I know you think that." He swallowed some of his drink. "Maybe you were right. Alice thinks I betrayed her but she's wrong. All I ever did was love her.

Perhaps I was wrong to do that." He finished the drink. "Anyway, it's over. Over and done with."

He ordered another drink and talked bitterly about how unfair she had been to him when he hadn't done anything to deserve it. Finishing his drink he got up.

"Where are you going, Steve?" Rachel asked him.

"To the office."

"May I come with you?"

He stood looking at her, his dark eyes intense, brooding. At last he shrugged. "Sure, Rachel. Why not?"

YOU CAN NOW ORDER PREVIOUS TITLES OF *SOAPS & SERIALS*™ BOOKS BY MAIL

Just complete the order form and detach on the dotted line and send together with your check or money order payable to **SOAPS & SERIALS:**

SOAPS & SERIALS™
120 Brighton Road, Box 5201
Clifton, NJ 07015-5201

Please circle the books you wish to order:

THE YOUNG AND THE RESTLESS	BK # 1 2 3
DAYS OF OUR LIVES	1 2 3
GUIDING LIGHT	1 2 3
ANOTHER WORLD	1 2 3
AS THE WORLD TURNS	1 2 3
CAPITOL™	1 2 3
DALLAS™	1 2 3
KNOTS LANDING™	1 2 3

Each book is $2.50 ($3.25 in Canada).

Total number of books circled _____
@ $2.50   ($3.25 Canada) $_____

Sales tax (CT residents only) $_____

Shipping and Handling $_____.95

Total payment enclosed (checks or
money orders only) $_____

Name _____

Address _____ Apt. # _____

City _____

State _____ Zip _____

Telephone No. _____

AW3